Shattered Dreams

TARA CONRAD

HIS ONE HER ONLY PUBLISHING

Contents

Svetlana	1
Maxim (Ten Years Ago)	10
Svetlana	14
Maxim (Ten Years Ago)	20
Svetlana	25
Svetlana	31
Maxim (Ten Years Ago)	36
Svetlana	39
Svetlana	47
Svetlana	54
Svetlana	60
Maxim (Ten years ago)	67
Maxim (Ten years ago)	74
Maxim (Ten years ago)	78
Svetlana	82
Svetlana	87
Svetlana	96
Svetlana	102
Svetlana	107
Svetlana	112
Svetlana	116
Maxim	121
Alex	124
Brandon	128
Brandon	134
Alex	139
Svetlana	142
Brandon	146
Svetlana	149
Svetlana	153
Svetlana	157
Alex	162

Svetlana   166
Svetlana   170
Brandon   179
Svetlana   183
Brandon   191
Svetlana   196
Brandon   200
Svetlana   203

Also by Tara Conrad   207
About Tara   208
Acknowledgments   209

To those who've ever felt broken, this story is for you. For the moments you thought you couldn't go on, for the strength you didn't realize you had, and for the hope that love can mend even the most shattered hearts. Never stop fighting for your dreams.

Svetlana

It doesn't matter that I've been here for three years. I still feel small and inconsequential each time I stand in front of the Moscow State University campus's main building. The rich history and legendary stories surrounding the Soviet-era architecture are not lost on me. I still have to pinch myself to make sure I'm not dreaming. That I'm actually here, in Moscow, walking around on my own.

Well, almost on my own. The only way I was able to convince Papa to allow me to live on campus was if Pyotr, one of his guards, came with me. It shouldn't have surprised me. Pyotr has been my personal detail since I was a young girl. The last thing I wanted was for him to have to follow me to university. I was worried I'd stick out and be ostracized, but I should've known better. Pyotr is well practiced at when to be by my side and when to be discreet.

Papa had assumed I'd stay close to home and attend St. Petersburg University. He should've known I wouldn't do things the way he anticipated. But, after the shock wore off, Papa was elated knowing I took his advice and was pursuing a business degree.

For the past few years, Papa's been grooming me to step into a leadership role at Jelena's Hope after college graduation. It's a dream I thought I shared, but after completing two years in the business program, I waivered in my resolve. Without consulting Papa, I changed my major at the start of this year—something I'm still not sure how to explain to my parents. Which is one of the topics that keep me coming to room 207 each week. When I arrive, I find the door open, a sign that Masha's not with another client.

"Good afternoon, Lana," Masha says when I enter her office.

"Hello again." I close the door, hang my backpack on the coat rack, and sit on her leather couch. Sure, it's a bit cliché, but it's worn in and super comfortable. Given the topics of conversation, I'll take any comfort I can get while I'm here.

"How's your week been so far?"

"It's going well." I can't hide my smile when I think about the recent events that have made each day better than the one before.

"You seem more upbeat than usual."

"A few weeks ago, I bumped into someone I know from back home."

"Would you care to elaborate on that?"

"Not yet." I'm already at odds with Czarenah, my mentor in the BDSM lifestyle. Even though Masha isn't usually judgmental, I'm not prepared to discuss Slava with anyone else yet.

"I'm here if and when you're ready." She pulls out her notebook and pen. "Shall we pick up where we left off last time?"

"I guess so." Until now, we've only covered the easy parts of my past—the happier memories. Last week, we ran out of time right before the awful day when everything changed. This is a big part of why I'm here, so I take a deep breath, forcing myself to return to the past. "It was the day before New Year's Eve. I was ten years old and still believed in Ded Moroz. I was so excited I couldn't contain my energy running round and round Papa's office." I smile and shake my head. "I was probably driving him crazy."

"Papa, may I mail Ded Moroz another letter?" I tug on his arm.

"Did you not already send him three letters?"

"*I did. But—*" *I hold up an envelope that's addressed and decorated. "—I forgot something."*

Papa smiles as he stands and walks out from behind his big desk. Although I'm interrupting his work, again, he never raises his voice or gets angry with me.

"Come moya babochka." Papa leads me out of his office. I take two steps to keep up with each of his. "Where is your sister?"

"She's in the library." Jelena's five years older than me, and she's super smart. She wants to be a doctor, just like Mama. When we're on break from school, instead of playing and having fun, she spends all her time in our library reading. Mama says I should be more like Jelena, but who wants to read books when they can play and enjoy the school holidays.

"Jelena," Papa says as he steps into the room. "Would you mind taking your sister to the post?"

"Of course not," Jelena says as she sets her book on the table. She and Papa exchange smiles as she walks toward us. "Another letter to Ded Moroz?"

"Yes. And it is her last letter. Is it not, Svetlana?"

"Yes, Papa."

"Thank you, malen'kiy tsvetok." Papa kisses Jelena on the head and goes back to his office.

"Come on, let's start bundling up."

Outside our window, snow's falling, and I'm certain it's freezing. But none of that matters. The only thing I care about is getting my most important request to Ded Moroz.

I would've been perfectly happy to throw on my coat and leave. Anything to mail my letter out as fast as possible. But Jelena is much too responsible for that and won't leave the house until we've put on our snow boots, hats, scarves, mittens, and heavy coats. It takes forever for us to get our winter gear on. But finally, we're properly dressed and on our way.

"What have you asked for this time?"

"A puppy."

"You know Papa won't let you have a puppy."

"That's why I'm not asking Papa. I'm asking Ded Moroz." I say as I skip down the sidewalk.

Jelena laughs softly. "Hopefully, that works."

"It will. I know it will. Papa can't say no to Ded Moroz."

"We got to the post office just as Radomir, the post worker, was closing up," I recall. "I knocked on the glass door with my mittened hand and held up the envelope."

With a smile on his face, Radomir walks towards us and unlocks the door. "What a pleasant surprise this is. What can I do for you today, Svetlana?"

"You must have visited the post office frequently if the employee knew your name?" Masha asks.

"Everyone in our community knew us because of Papa. But that holiday, I did spend a lot of time at the post."

"I have an important letter to mail."

"Well, then, you best come in, and I'll get it posted for you right away."

"Are you coming?" I ask Jelena.

She looks up from her phone. "I'll wait out here. You go ahead."

I shrug and follow Radomir inside.

"Do you have another letter for Ded Moroz?" he asks.

"Yep. I forgot to ask him for a puppy."

"I see," he says as he puts the stamps on my envelope and holds it up for my approval before placing it in the mail bin. "I hope you get your wish."

"I'm sure I will."

Radomir walks me to the door. "Spokoynoy nochi."

"You, too." I smile as I walk back outside and look for Jelena.

She's not out front on the sidewalk where I left her. I look around, trying to find her. Listening closely, I hear voices around the side of the building. I don't want to be seen, so I walk as carefully as possible in that direction and take a quick look around the corner. Jelena is with Gavrill, and he's kissing her. Yuck.

I've snuck peeks at my older sister's diary and know she has a crush on Gavriil. Papa has forbidden her to see him because

Gavriil is the son of Rudolf Sergin, another Pakhan in the Bratva. Someone Papa does not do business with. Gavriil shouldn't even be in our community. It could cause a lot of problems.

I'm trying to stay hidden, but my nose gets that tingly feeling, the kind that happens right before I sneeze. I do my best to hold it in, but it's no use. I sneeze loudly and give myself away. Jelena and Gavriil both startle.

"Svetlana." Jelena hurries over to me, grabbing me by the arms. "Don't tell on me, please. I'll talk to Papa about getting you a puppy," she begs, trying to bribe me.

I look over her shoulder at the brown-haired boy who's leaning against the building. Gavriil stares back. His eyes are dark and frightening. I don't like him at all, but I'd never tattle on my sister. She's my best friend, and friends don't tell each other's secrets. "I won't say anything. I promise."

"Thank you." She grabs my hand, and we start for home.

As we walk away, I glance back and see Gavriil talking on the phone. Something about the way he's watching us doesn't feel right. Papa says I should always listen to that little voice inside.

"If we don't hurry, Papa's going to come looking for us." Jelena tugs on my arm, trying to get me to move faster, but I resist. I want to stay outside, not hurry home and be stuck indoors.

"I should have listened to her," I say. "We didn't even have a chance to argue about it because everything happened so fast. A van came out of nowhere and screeched to a stop in front of us." I close my eyes, and the memories play like a movie. "The back doors flew open, and two masked men jumped out."

One of the men grabs Jelena. He's wearing a mask, but his long, greasy hair pokes out of the sides. "Svetlana, run," she yells.

"Let her go," I scream, trying to go to her, but the other man grabs me. I nearly gag at the smell of vodka on his breath.

"Leave her," the greasy-haired guy says.

Vodka breath pushes me to the ground, but I jump up, knowing I have to save my sister.

"Lana, run. Go get Papa." Jelena's fighting as hard as she can. Kicking and punching. Anything to avoid being pulled into the van.

I don't want to leave my sister, but she's right. These guys are too big for me to fight. I'm too far from home and won't get to Papa fast enough. I look around, hoping there's someone who'll help us. In the next block up, there's a group of people getting out of a car. I'm sure they'll help me. I run as fast as I can.

"Help," I call, but when they see what's going on, they turn away and hurry into their house, closing the door. "No." I try to scream, but nothing comes out. I'm left standing helpless on the sidewalk with tears pouring down my face.

Even though it's been ten years, the visceral memories of that day are so powerful I catch myself holding my breath from the intensity of my emotions. "I don't know how or why, but I could hear Papa's voice in my head reminding me to pay attention and memorize every detail. So, that's what I did. I memorized as many details as I could and then ran home." I wipe the tears that are sliding down my cheeks. "To this day, I still can't stand the smell of vodka."

"Papa. Papa," I call through my tears as I burst in the front door.

"What is it?" he asks as he rushes from his office.

"It's Jelena. Men took her."

Papa gets down to my level. "What do you mean?"

"We were coming home. There was a van. Men jumped out," I choke on a sob. "They took Jelena."

Papa stands up and turns to Misha, "Gather a team, now."

"Yes, sir."

I was so focused on telling Papa what happened that I didn't hear Mama come in, but now she's standing beside me crying. "Oh God, Maxim," she whispers.

"Moya vozlyublenny," Papa says and puts his arms around Mama. "I will find our daughter and bring her home." Then, he turns to me. "Svetlana, go to my office. I will be right there."

While I wait, I take off my coat and boots. I repeat the details in my head the entire time so I don't forget them. It doesn't take long for Papa, followed by Misha and a few other guards, to come into the office. Papa sits in his big chair and motions for me to go to him.

"I need you to be a brave girl right now and tell me everything you remember."

"Jelena and I were walking home. She wanted me to hurry, but I was giving her a hard time. I wanted to stay outside." My tears fall faster. "I should've listened to her."

"It's okay, moya babochka," Papa reassures me. "What happened next?"

As hard as it is, I tell Papa how the men jumped out and dragged her away. That there were people. I called out to them, but they hurried into their house. "Why wouldn't they help us?"

"How many men were there?" Misha asks.

"I saw three. Two men grabbed us, and another man was driving. He had a hat on, but I couldn't see what it said."

"Do you remember anything else about them?"

"The man who grabbed Jelena had greasy black hair. The other man, the one who grabbed me, smelled yucky, like vodka."

"Could you see their faces?"

"They had black masks on. The kind that all the boys wear when we're playing in the snow," I say.

"Did they have any scars or tattoos?" Papa asks.

"The man who grabbed me had tattoos on his hand." I think hard, trying to remember exactly what they looked like. "There was an ugly pig with horns. Next to it were some dots. And there were three crosses."

"You're doing great, Lana," Misha praises me. "Just a few more questions, ok? I nod. "What did the van look like?"

"It was white, and it was old and rusty. When the back doors opened, they creaked really loud. And there were no windows."

"Do you remember the license plate?"

I close my eyes again, trying to picture the van. "I don't think there was one."

"That should be enough for us to start looking," Misha says. "Do you need anything else from us, boss?"

"No. I'll be over as soon as I'm done here." Misha and the men begin to file out of the room.

Guilt gnaws at me, knowing I haven't said everything. I don't want to break my promise to Jelena, but I have to tell Papa. "Wait," I call. Everyone stops and looks at me. "There's one more thing. Gavrill was at the post."

"Gavriil? What was he doing there?"

"He and Jelena were talking." Fresh tears trickle down my cheeks, knowing I betrayed my sister by telling her secret. I curl into him, needing the safety of Papa's hug.

"Find the boy," Papa barks out the order.

"I'm on it." Then, they disappear from the room.

"I shouldn't have left her, Papa."

He holds me away from him so I can see his face. "You did the right thing, moya babochka." He kisses my forehead and then stands. "Go to your Mama. I will find your sister and bring her home. Do not worry."

"Even though I was young and didn't understand the extent of the evil at play, something inside me knew I'd never see my sister again."

"That must have been very scary. Especially for such a little girl."

"It was the most terrifying day of my life."

"Given the traumatic events of the day. How did you remember so many details? Most adults wouldn't have had the composure to manage that."

"You have to understand how we were raised. Our lives were never what anyone would consider *normal*. Danger's inherent in Papa's line of work. From a young age, the need to be aware and pay attention to details was drilled into our heads."

"It seems your parents' efforts were successful."

"I guess." I shrug.

"You guess?"

"I mean, yes, I remembered a lot of details. But there's always been one thing I could never understand."

"What is that?"

"They had us both, but they let me go. Why?" My body begins trembling. "Why didn't they take me, too?"

"Many people have similar feelings after experiencing a traumatic event. It's called survivor's guilt."

"I need to stop."

"Okay. Close your eyes and take some deep breaths." I try to relax and focus on my breathing. "Svetlana, you have the power over your memories and emotions. It's okay to put those into a safe place until our next session."

After a few more breaths, I open my eyes. "I'm okay now." I get up and grab my backpack.

"If you need anything, I don't care what time it is, call or text me."

"I will."

As I leave the office, I push the horrific memories as deep as they'll go, trading them for the anticipation of what's to come tonight.

Maxim (Ten Years Ago)

"Papa, Papa." The desperate plea in Svetlana's cry has me running from my office with Misha right on my heels.

"What is it?" My heart pounds as though it already knows what my daughter is about to say.

"It's Jelena. Men took her." Those words are something no parent is ever prepared to hear. I stoop down in front of Svetlana. "What do you mean?"

"We were coming home. There was a van. Men jumped out." She is crying and out of breath. "They took Jelena."

I stand and turn to Misha, "Gather a team, now."

"Yes, sir." Misha wastes no time. He is already on his phone giving orders to my men.

Irina has just made her way down the steps and is now standing next to our daughter. Tears are pouring down her face. "Oh God, Maxim." Her voice is barely audible.

Rage and fear are boiling inside me, but I cannot let my wife or daughter see my barely controlled emotions. "Moya vozlyublenny." I wrap my arms around my wife's trembling body. "I will find our daughter and bring her home." I turn to Svetlana. "Go to my office. I will be right there." Before I do anything else, I must comfort my wife.

"Oh, Maxim," Irina cries. "You have to find her."

"I will not rest until I do." I hold her to me, not only comforting her but also using her physical closeness to ground my rapidly fraying emotions. "I will not allow harm to come to Jelena. You must trust me."

She nods and then pulls away. "You shouldn't be wasting time on me. Go and find our daughter."

I hurry back to my office, knowing every second we are not out searching for Jelena is a second wasted.

My daughter has impressed me with the amount of information she was able to retain. She's shown courage well beyond her years. If not for the details she gave us, we would not know where to start. I dismiss Misha and the rest of my men so they can get ready to go.

Once we are alone, Svetlana lays her head on my shoulder, and her little body trembles in my arms. "I shouldn't have left her, Papa."

I pick up her tiny frame and hold her so I can see her face. "You did the right thing, *moya babochka*." I kiss her forehead and set her on her feet. "Go to your Mama. I will find your sister and bring her home. Do not worry." I watch as she runs up the steps and disappears down the hallway before I hurry in the other direction to get to work.

With each step, I allow the burning rage to become my driving force. When I get to my command room, I find only Misha waiting for me.

"Where is everyone?"

"Timur and Igor are already out looking for Gavriil, and I have two other teams deployed to search Sergin's warehouses."

The world I live and work in is dangerous. That is a fact I have never ignored. However, in my world, there have always been rules. One of which is that women and children are off-limits. Rudolf Sergin does not seem to abide by such rules. He has blind-sided me and stolen something very precious to me.

"Fuck," I yell and swipe my arm across the table, sending everything flying. I grab the edge of the round black table in the center of the room and drop my head. I have never been in a situation like this. For the first time in my life, I am terrified.

"Boss." Misha places his hand on my shoulder. "We *will* find her."

I lift my head and meet his stare. "I do not care how many people die. We will find my daughter," I growl. I check my weapon, ensuring it is fully loaded, and slide it back into the waistband of my pants. With barely controlled rage, I press my finger against the sensor, unlocking the weapons room. I grab a second semi-automatic gun and holster, securing it in place.

"What are you doing?"

"What does it look like?" I do not stop loading up with as much ammunition as I can carry.

"You aren't coming out. Not like this."

"The fuck I am not. Jelena is my daughter. I am not sitting home when she is out there somewhere."

"Boss, I don't think—"

"Move the hell out of my way, or I will not be responsible for what happens next."

Misha must sense the seriousness of my words because he steps out of my way. "The Escalade is out front. I'll drive."

I am getting into the passenger seat when movement catches my eye. Svetlana is standing on the porch. "Go back in the house," I bark out the order, but she does not move. I do not like my little girl seeing me for what I truly am—a killer. Slamming my door closed, I turn to Misha. "Go."

I watch her in the mirror as we drive away. My heart shatters as she wraps her arms around her little body and drops to her knees. I force myself to look away, knowing Irina is there to take care of her while I am gone to bring Jelena home.

Svetlana

PYOTR IS WAITING IN HIS USUAL SPOT, A WOODEN bench against a wall overlooking the opulent rotunda. Bright sunlight shines through the opaque skylights surrounding a stained-glass star, representing the old Soviet Union. I don't know how the echoing of footsteps and voices doesn't drive him crazy. I watch him for several minutes, impressed by his constant state of awareness. It's only because of his presence that I can relax, knowing he's in control. Even though I fought Papa when he insisted my childhood guard accompany me to university, I can't lie. I'm glad he's here.

Pyotr gets up when he sees me coming. "All done?"

"I am."

"Do you have plans for tonight?" The expression on his face implores me to say no, that I'm staying in. But he knows me better than that.

"Actually, I do." I grin.

"I don't like that look."

"Slava is in town. He'll be picking me up at seven."

"Is he taking you to Ecstasy?"

"He is." And I can't wait. We're going to be doing a scene together.

Shortly after I turned eighteen, I approached my parents with questions about the BDSM lifestyle. My parents have been in a Dominant/submissive relationship for many years. Mama modeled the grace and selflessness of a submissive, while Papa was an example of stern yet loving leadership. They never hid their involvement in the lifestyle from me, but like any other couple, they didn't share what went on behind closed doors.

Most of my friends would never have approached their parents with such a question. So many families in my country are still very patriarchal and don't allow such openness. But my parents are different. They are open and willing to answer any questions I have.

It didn't surprise them that I would be interested in the lifestyle. Although Mama joked that she never thought I would be curious about submission. She assumed that with my more *assertive* tendencies, being a dominant might be more appealing to me. For a brief moment, I considered it. Except the idea of being responsible for another person didn't interest me. Mama gave me an e-reader loaded with several quality books about the lifestyle and asked me to read them before we took any further steps.

When I showed continued interest, Mama brought me to Noire, the dungeon she and Papa go to. She introduced me to Czarenah, another experienced submissive who would become my mentor. Where my parents and I have an open relationship, discussing specifics about their sex life or mine is not a topic either of us is comfortable with. I've enjoyed learning from Czarenah and consider her almost like a second mother. Currently, we have a difference of opinions, though.

Shortly after I moved to Moscow, I started the search for a BDSM dungeon. It didn't take long to find Ecstasy. I've been going there a few times a month for the past three years. There have been several occasions that I agreed to scene with a Dominant, but mostly, I'm just here to watch. That's what I was doing last weekend when a man sat in the chair next to me.

"Excuse me, are you Svetlana Solonik?"

The use of my full name startled me. But when I turned my head, I saw a familiar face. "Slava?"

"I thought that was you." He smiles.

"What are you doing here?"

"I'm in town on business. I read about this place while I was online looking for a club in the area. I thought I'd stop in."

Slava's a Dominant I recognize from Noire. We seemed to hit it off and spent the evening talking. The club was closing for the night, but we weren't ready to say goodbye. So, we found a local bar and had a few drinks. Before parting ways, we exchanged numbers. There was a text waiting for me the following day. Slava wanted to know if I'd like to do a scene with him next weekend. Of course, I said yes.

I dated a lot in high school, but once I started mentoring, I stopped pursuing men who weren't in the lifestyle. During my training, I was able to play with a few of the Dominants at Noire, who helped train new submissives. Several Dominants had expressed an interest in me outside of our training scene. At the time, Czarenah didn't feel I was ready for anything outside of that strictly controlled environment.

In my opinion, everything's different now. I've grown and gained more experience. After I hung up with Slava, I couldn't wait to call Czarenah and share my excitement with her. But, instead of being happy, she was the ultimate buzzkill. She expressed her strong disapproval of me even playing with Slava. Czarenah felt our age difference and my lack of experience are potential red flags. Both were things I disagreed strongly with. Slava is a respected and experienced Dominant. Which, to me, makes him the perfect candidate.

"I assume he's picking you up again?" Pyotr asks as we walk back to my dorm building.

"He is."

"I'll follow you in our car."

"You can stay home, you know. I'm safe with Slava."

"And have your father murder me when he finds out? Not a chance."

I laugh as I put the key into the lock of my dorm room door. "He wouldn't have to find out."

"Not going to happen, little butterfly." His mouth cracks in a rare smile. "I'll stay out of your way, but I will be there."

"You should get yourself a submissive while we're there. It might do you some good." I hurry into my room and close the door before he has a chance to respond.

I'm still in the shower, rinsing my hair when my cell rings. I'm expecting a call from Slava, so I reach out and swipe to connect the call and put it on speaker.

"Hello?"

"Hi," Czarenah says. "Do you have a few minutes to talk?"

"Can you hang on one second?"

"Sure."

I regret not checking the screen before I answered. The last thing I want right now is another argument about not seeing Slava. I hurry and throw a towel around me.

"Sorry about that. I was finishing washing my hair."

"Are you going out tonight?"

"Yes." I may as well get this out of the way since I'm sure this is why she's calling. "Slava will be here in an hour."

"Is there any way I can talk some sense into you?"

"What's that supposed to mean?"

"Slava was at the dungeon earlier this week. He and I had the opportunity to discuss you."

"Okay." I start combing my hair out, partially ignoring her.

"I already told Slava my feelings, and now I'm going to tell you. I don't think it's the right time for you to move forward with him."

"I disagree with you."

"Tell me why you disagree?"

"I don't mean any disrespect. You've taught me well, but I've spent enough time being a student. I'm ready to find an interested Dominant and begin vetting."

"May I explain my point of view?"

"I guess." I'm glad we're on the telephone so she can't see me roll my eyes. I'm certain Czarenah's going to tell me I'm too young. Too inexperienced. But how can one gain experience if they don't get the chance to try?

"This is the first time you're living on your own."

"It's been three years."

"Yes, but you've also just started trauma therapy. You've worked at Jelena's Hope. You understand that as you begin to work through what you've experienced, you'll likely experience many strong emotions. Ones that may cloud your vision. I've known Slava for a long time, and although he's a trustworthy Dominant—"

"Shouldn't that make this a good move?" I interrupt.

"In ordinary circumstances, yes. But what you are going through is far from ordinary. I don't want to see you make decisions that may be clouded by feelings and emotions. It could end badly for both you and Slava. I'm begging you to give yourself some more time."

Czarenah's come to mean a lot to me both as a mentor and a friend. I've always welcomed her advice. Which makes what I'm about to do that much harder. "I can't thank you enough for everything you've taught me. You've made sure I'm prepared for this next part of my journey as a submissive," I say and clear my throat, hoping to hold back the tears that threaten to fall. "But if you're not going to support me with this, I think it's best to part ways."

"Svetlana, please. Don't shut me out."

"I have to go. Slava will be here shortly, and I don't want to keep him waiting."

"Is there anything I can say to get you to wait?"

"You've been very good to me, and I hate that things are ending this way. But I refuse to walk away from Slava without exploring what's between us."

"I see. I'll be here if you need anything."

"Goodbye, Czarenah." I disconnect the call.

Czarenah's made her case, and we're no longer on the same page. I know she thinks I'm being stubborn and reckless. She'll probably run right to Papa, but I don't care. I'm no longer a child. I'm an adult who's fully capable of making her own decisions. She and I have come to an impasse, and it's time for us to go our separate ways.

How long does she expect me to watch from the sidelines before I take the next logical step—beginning to vet a Dominant. And why not Slava? We didn't seek one another out. It happened by chance. I like to think fate had a part in bringing us together. He's well-known and respected in the community. To me, it only makes sense that if we're interested in playing or having a dynamic, we should be able to do so without interference.

Maxim (Ten Years Ago)

From the moment Jelena was taken, we have been one step behind—a position I do not like to be in. If not for Svetlana's ability to retain so many vital details—No. I cannot think about the disadvantages we would face. Knowing Gavriil and his father are involved is a crucial piece of the puzzle. Unfortunately, Rudolf Sergin has left nothing to chance. Within minutes after Svetlana mentioned Gavriil's name, my men were out looking for him. Being the son of a mob boss, he was able to disappear quickly. But no one can hide forever.

It took several hours, but Timur and Igor found the boy and brought him to one of my facilities. I intend to extract my daughter's whereabouts from him. Timur pulls into the gravel parking lot outside the building. I do not wait for the vehicle to come to a complete stop before throwing the door open. I storm into the room where they're holding Gavriil.

"Where is she, you son of a bitch?"

"Wouldn't you like to know," he laughs. "That bitch is one hot piece of ass."

My fist connects with his face. Blood splatters from his now broken nose.

"I am going to ask you one more time. Where is my daughter?"

Gavriil spits on my shoe, infuriating me. "You are a dead man." I pull the gun from my waistband, click off the safety, and aim at his head.

Timur hurries to my side. "Boss, if you kill him now, we'll never get the information we need." He keeps his voice low. What he says may be true, but I remain poised to kill. "Maxim, you're not thinking clearly. Take a step back, and let us handle this."

My body shakes with uncontrolled rage. Killing is part of my life. It is something I have done many times. If it is the choice between them or me, I will pull the trigger without hesitation. But I have never felt bloodthirsty. I have never been blinded by such hate that I long to pull the trigger—until now. I want the satisfaction of watching the life drain from this piece of shit in front of me. However, Timur is correct. Gavriil is the only link we have to Jelena's whereabouts. If I kill him, the trail will go cold. That is a chance I cannot take.

With a click, I put the safety back on and lower my weapon. "Do whatever you need to get him to talk." I give the order and then summon every ounce of self-control I possess to leave the room. I do not stop until I am in my makeshift office, where I call my wife.

"Did you find her?" she asks as soon as the line connects.

"Not yet. We are questioning Gavriil."

"Max, I'm so scared."

"I know, *vozlyublenny*." I am equally as scared, but I do my best to keep my voice calm and even. "Jelena will be back in our arms very soon. I need you to have faith." Faith enough for the two of us.

Sitting here alone, not knowing what is happening in the other room, is killing me. Several times, I have gone to the door with the intent to rejoin the questioning. But Timur was right. I am too close to this situation and will only hamper their efforts. I hire only the best men, a fact which I must trust.

It feels as though an eternity has passed before Misha walks into the office. "Where is she?" I ask, jumping to my feet.

"His father taught him well. He wasn't prepared to give up any information easily," Timur responds as he pulls his bloody T-shirt off and tosses it into the garbage before going into the closet to grab a clean shirt. "Once we employed some non-traditional methods, he broke quickly. The kid gave us two names—Valery and Boris. Says they're *brodyaga* in his father's organization."

"Where are they?"

"They landed in Serbia about two hours ago. Igor made a few calls and got footage from the security system at the Belgrade airport. We were able to confirm Jelena was with them." I grab my phone to call Irina. "I've already contacted Obrad Radovanović. He has boots on the ground tracking them."

I tap the green call button, and the line connects.

"Did you—"

"Have my bags packed. I am going to get our daughter."

Six hours later, the wheels of my jet touchdown on a private airstrip. Radovanović is waiting for us on the tarmac.

"It's good to see you, Solonik. Although, I wish it were under better circumstances."

"As do I."

We waste no time walking to waiting vehicles. While we walk, Radovanović fills me in on the progress his foot soldiers have made. "We tracked the men and your daughter to a holding facility. I was with my team when they arrived, but we were too late. They were already gone."

"Chert voz'mi." We have been doing everything right, yet they continue to slip out of our grasp.

"They're traveling amidst a known trafficking ring," he explains as we get into the back of his black Mercedes S Class. Misha rides in the front with the driver. "That is both a good and bad thing."

"How much do you know about the group?" Misha asks.

"We know the operation and have been on their trail for years. Each time we find a warehouse, we close it down. But they are very organized and have underground networks of their own."

Misha's cell rings. "It's Timur." While Misha is on the phone, Radovanović shares more information about this trafficking ring.

"Where are we?" I interrupt him when the car stops in front of a tall wrought iron gate.

"This is my home."

"What are we doing here? I need to be out searching for my daughter."

"Our combined forces will continue searching. But you are exhausted. You need a few hours of sleep and a good meal."

"Like hell I do," I argue. There is no way I can rest while my daughter is out there, alone.

"Maxim, you cannot go after these men when you are distracted by physical exhaustion." He gets out of the car and waits for me to follow. "You must trust in our men."

"Jelena is my daughter. I need to be out there," I yell and step closer to Radovanović, preparing to challenge him.

"You will be out there as soon as you can think straight." He remains calm despite my anger. "I have known you for many years, Solonik. I can tell when you're off your game. If you go out there like this, you'll get yourself or someone else killed."

I do not want to admit his observation is correct. I am so tired I cannot form a clear thought. I am reacting instead of responding, something I always warn my men against. That is when mistakes are made. "Fine. An hour. Then I join the search." I concede.

We spend the next three weeks chasing in Serbia, chasing Jelena and her captures around the country. Each time we believe we are closing in on them, they outsmart us and get away.

Tonight's intel is solid. Jelena was seen at this location, which turns out to be no more than a flophouse, this morning. Hopes are high that tonight, the tables are about to turn in our favor. I am ready to have my daughter safely back in my arms.

I know we are too late as soon as we breach the entrance and are not met with resistance.

"Boss. Up here," Misha calls from a room on the second floor.

I hurry up the steps, hoping my assessment is wrong and that he has Jelena. But that hope is gone when I find Misha holding the pink sweater Jelena was wearing the day she was taken. He hands me the now dirty sweater that is still warm from being worn. "Fuck," I roar.

"What's wrong?" Timur rushes into the room with Radovanović on his heels.

I hold the sweater close to me. "She was just here. We are too late again."

We go back downstairs and meet up with Radovanović's men, who are returning inside. "We found an underground tunnel in the shed. I sent a group down to track them." He looks to his boss. "These tunnel systems are intricate. They could be anywhere."

Tonight was supposed to be the night. Jelena should be with me on my jet, flying home. Instead, the trail has gone cold, and I am returning home empty-handed. As much as I do not want to leave Serbia, I am confident they are no longer here. We are back to square one, relying on technology to locate them. This part of the work can be done from my home.

I hold onto Jelena's sweater. It is a reminder of how close we got. It is a hope that she is still alive and a prayer that next time, we will find her.

Svetlana

Ecstasy is packed. The energy from the people in attendance is electric.

"Are we going to do a public scene tonight?"

"No."

"Why not?"

"It is our first scene together," he explains. "I want us to have privacy to take things at a slower pace rather than being concerned with putting a show for the onlookers." I'm disappointed, but I'm afraid he'll back out of the scene if I argue. "I've reserved a room if you're ready."

Slava takes my hand and guides me up the stairs to the club's second floor, where the private rooms are located. Although I've played with a few Dominants at this club, this time feels very different. I went into those scenes knowing it was a one-and-done deal. Tonight, all options are on the table. The door closes behind us, blocking out the thumping bass from the music in the main room. Now it's just Slava and me.

"Sit down. We need to go over the rules first."

My heels click on the polished concrete floor as I make my way to the leather sofa. Slava follows, sitting next to me. I've never been in any of the private rooms Ecstasy offers. I take a minute to admire the room's ultra-modern design with minimalist furniture and clean lines. Three walls are covered in creamy white textured wallpaper, while the wall behind the black metal bed is painted a deep purple. Against the wall across from the bed are glass shelves. Various paddles, crops, floggers, canes, and whips are laid out neatly on the shelves. The ceiling boasts several skylights that, during the day, would allow for natural light. Tonight, the recessed lights are dimmed, adding to the dark and dangerous feel of the room.

"Do you have any experience with impact play?"

"Yes. While I was mentoring under Czarenah, I expressed a desire to experiment with it. She oversaw several interactions with a Dominant who introduced me to each implement."

"What were your conclusions?"

"It was a few strikes with each, but I enjoyed it very much."

"Good." He smiles. "Let's discuss limits."

"I don't have any," I answer quickly.

Slava snickers. "*Moya nevinnyy malysh*, I can assure you that you do have limits."

"I guess I haven't encountered them yet." I shrug.

"I will tell you my limits. I feel comfortable using a flogger, crop, or paddle. Whips and canes are off the table."

"Why?"

"You don't have a good gauge on where your limits lie."

He nods. "How do you feel about bondage?"

"I've never experienced it."

"This will be a good first, then. Do you have anything you'd like to request?"

"Yes. I want to be blindfolded and gagged."

He studies me for a moment. "Why?"

"I want to experience everything."

"I'm not comfortable with that tonight."

"Why not?" I want this. I need this.

"I get a great deal of pleasure giving a willing submissive pain. However, your inexperience and this being the first time we're playing together is not the time for experimenting with such extremes. I've seen it too many times. An eager sub who doesn't know their limits or who wishes to impress their Dominant agrees to more than they're going to be able to handle. Oftentimes, they don't safeword for fear of disappointing the Dominant or ending a scene." He pauses.

"I've also witnessed the aftermath of physical and emotional injuries. I've witnessed both Dominants and submissives leave the lifestyle because of the damage done. I don't want that for you. After this scene, I want you begging for me."

"You have years of experience. Doesn't that make me safe with you?"

"Ah, *moya nevinnyy malysh*. I will do everything in my power to keep you safe, but I'm only human. I can't foresee everything and refuse to leave your safety to chance. Do you agree to my limits?"

"Yes, Sir."

Slava sets safewords, and once he's sure we're on the same page, he gives his command. "Strip and kneel."

I bring my hand to the zipper on the front of my dress. His eyes follow as I drag the zipper down slowly, allowing the fabric to slip from my arms, landing on the floor by my feet. The corner of his mouth lifts in a smile as he takes in my naked body. I lower myself to kneel before him. Slava stands and steps closer to me.

"You like to be the one calling the shots, and you challenge anyone who tries to strip that control from you." He gently strokes my hair. "Tonight, I'm going to show you just how good giving up that control can be."

I have to force myself not to move. Slava's assessment of me is spot on. But I plan to show him I can submit to his demands yet remain in complete control. He unbuttons his dark blue dress shirt and disappears from my sight line.

I can hear his footsteps and other sounds behind me. I'm certain he's gathering items for our scene. Given his questions, I'm assuming we're doing something with impact, but he's not laid out the exact details. My mind races, trying to come up with possible scene ideas.

"Stand and come to me," he orders.

I rise from the floor, mindful of being graceful, and walk over to where Slava stands next to the bed. That's when I get my first glimpse of him, and what I imagined is nothing compared to what I see. His upper body has well-defined muscles that lead to a lean chest and abs. I follow the trail of dark hair that dips below the waistband of his jeans. My tongue runs across my lower lip, seeing the outline of his erection.

"Put your arms out in front of you." Slava reaches around me to the bed. "This is bondage tape. If, for any reason, you are uncomfortable and need to stop the scene, I can have it off in seconds."

"Yes, Sir."

He wraps the thin plastic-like material around my wrists. It's not sticky, and it adheres only to itself.

"Are you ready to give control over to me?"

I drop my gaze, unable to answer him.

"Look at me." Slowly, I bring my head back up. "When I ask a question, I expect an answer. Are you ready to give control over to me?"

"No, Sir."

"No?" He raises an eyebrow. "Are you certain you want to proceed with this scene?"

"Yes, Sir."

"Bend over the bed and put your arms above your head." Slava nudges my legs apart and lands his first strike. He continues spanking me with his open hand. "Your skin is the most beautiful shade of pink. Now that you're sufficiently warmed up, let's try something more impactful."

There's a swoosh and then a stinging sensation across my upper thighs.

"How does that feel?"

"It stings. I like it."

He continues alternating between my thighs and my ass. Just as the sting begins to morph into numbness, he stops.

Slava's hand cups my pussy. "Are you wet for me, *moya nevinnyy malysh?*"

I nod, and he removes his touch.

"Are you wet for me?" he asks again.

"Yes, Sir. I am."

He drags two fingers through my folds before plunging them inside my center. I'm so turned on by the spanking that I moan from the small amount of contact. He continues dragging them in and out until I'm a panting mess. Then, they disappear. I groan from the loss of contact.

The next strike is an unexpected thuddy sensation. Slava alternates sides as he increases the intensity.

"You need to relax," he instructs.

"I can't," I argue.

Strike.

"You can."

Strike.

"No." I grit my teeth, trying to hold on to the last shreds of my control.

"Why not?" I gasp at the intensity of the next strike.

"Because I don't want to."

Strike.

"I don't believe that," Slava challenges me. "I think there's more to it."

"I can't give up control."

"Why not, Svetlana?"

"I'm afraid."

The paddle connects with my flesh hard and fast.

"I'll keep you safe. You don't have to be afraid."

"It's too much."

"What's your color?"

"Green."

"Give in to me."

"I don't know how." Almost without my consent, my body begins to relax into each strike, embracing the pain.

"That's it." His voice sounds far away. Although I hear the noise of the paddle connecting with my body, I no longer feel the pain. "Let go, *moya nevinnyy malysh.*"

Everything has faded away, and I'm weightless. The constant thoughts in my head are silent. There's no pain or fear. I want to stay here forever.

"Svetlana. It's time to wake up now."

I blink a few times, trying to get my body to comply. Finally, my eyes open, and Slava's face comes into focus. I'm captivated by the deep blue in his eyes.

"Welcome back."

"What happened?"

"You finally allowed yourself to give in and allow me to have control." He smiles. "And you experienced subspace."

Tears begin falling. "I don't know why I'm crying."

"It's the extremes of the emotions you've just experienced." He reaches out and pulls me close to him. "Stay the night with me. Allow me to care for you."

I agree to return to his hotel, where he spends the night and the entirety of the following day, tending to my every need. He's tender and kind, ensuring I'm not only physically but emotionally cared for.

It's so difficult to walk out of his room knowing he wants me to stay with him again. Unfortunately, I have a presentation for school I need to finish working on.

Svetlana

"How was your weekend?" Masha asks as I take my usual seat in her office.

"It was good." I keep my voice calm and don't go into detail. I'm not ready to dissect what may be developing between Slava and myself.

"Where would you like to start today?"

"I guess we should pick up where I left off."

"As long as you're comfortable with that."

I wouldn't say I'm comfortable, but it seems to be what makes the most sense. I take a deep breath and adjust my position on the couch as my thoughts transport me back in time.

"Over the next few weeks, our lives became even more unrecognizable. Papa hired triple the number of guards for our property. The little time he was home, he spent in his office with the door closed. Most of the time, he was out with his men searching for Jelena.

Mama was home but very much gone at the same time. I could hear her crying when I walked by her bedroom door. I tried to open it several times but couldn't find the courage to do so. How was I supposed to look her in the eyes, knowing I stood by and watched while those men took Jelena away?"

"Hey, kiddo," Dimitri says, sitting beside me on the stairs.

"Dimitri's my cousin," I explain. "He was staying with us for a few weeks before he had to return to Ukraine to serve his conscription."

"I see," she says and jots some notes down.

"Hi," I mumble.

"What are you doing?"

"Sitting."

"I see that." He elbows me jokingly. "Why are you sitting on the steps?" I shrug. "I can see something's wrong." I continue counting the marble tiles on the foyer floor while I debate telling him what's bothering me. "Your secret's safe with me."

"I was in the kitchen with Olga when Misha and the other guards brought Gavrill back here." I was in the kitchen helping Olga get dinner ready. We were peeling potatoes when the SUV stopped, and I froze with the potato peeler in my hand. I couldn't take my eyes off the scene outside the window. "When Olga saw what I was watching, she shooed me from the kitchen. Told me I was slowing her down too much."

"I see."

"Gavriil was handcuffed and beat up." I look at Dimitri. "Papa's going to kill him, isn't he?"

"Of course not." Dimitri's voice rises an octave, giving away his lie.

Masha holds her hand up, stopping me. "Was this the first time you witnessed something like this?"

"My papa having someone brought to our property?"

"Yes."

"It was. Papa never hid what he did from us, but he also didn't allow business to be conducted in our presence. I wasn't meant to see it this time either, but no one knew I was in the kitchen."

"That's a lot of violence for a young girl. How did it make you feel?"

I don't answer for several minutes. I never stopped to think about how seeing that made me feel. "Regardless of what Papa's job is, I always knew he was a good man. He would never set out to hurt innocent people. Gavriil wasn't innocent, and Papa was only doing what was necessary."

"You've explained your knowledge of your Papa's business," Masha says in her usual calm manner. "But you didn't say how it made you feel."

"I don't really know." I shrug. "I've always been immensely proud of Papa. He could do no wrong in my eyes. And Gavriil. Just saying his name brings back my all-consuming hatred for him."

"I'm not a baby, Dimitri. Gavriil was involved with Jelena's kidnapping, and now Papa's going to kill him."

Dimitri sighs. "We shouldn't be talking about this."

"Why not?"

"You're a girl. You're not involved in Maxim's business."

All the emotions I've been trying to avoid boil over, and I shoot up. "I'm not involved?" I yell. "I was with Jelena when they grabbed her. It was me who ran and left her to be taken. But you think I'm not involved?"

Dimitri takes my hand. "I'm sorry. Those weren't the right words. I just meant that your papa doesn't want you affected by the things he has to do."

"Well, it's too late. I'm already affected."

"Those were some pretty big feelings for a little girl."

"I really believed my parents blamed me for Jelena's disappearance, and that's why they were avoiding me."

"You were very close to your parents. Those feelings of alienation must have been difficult."

"I was close to them. Then, almost overnight, they weren't there anymore." I wipe a tear from my cheek and take a second to compose myself. "The new year came and signaled a great deal of change for me. I wasn't a foolish child making wishes to a fairy tale character. I did a lot of growing up and realized such things didn't exist. What did exist were the nightmares I had about my sister being snatched from my side."

I look up at Masha, who's no longer writing. Instead, she's watching me intently while I tell my story. "A piece of my childhood was stolen when Jelena was taken. My childhood, the time of viewing the world through naïve eyes, was over. I started seeing the world as it truly is—cruel and unforgiving. I realized I could never return to the person I was before that day."

Papa got in late last night. Something I wished for because today's my eleventh birthday. Mama and Papa always make a big deal out of our birthdays. We get a special breakfast and a big party. I wasn't expecting a party this year. I don't need a party. I'll be happy to get to spend the day with my parents. I race downstairs to the dining room for my special birthday breakfast with my parents. But when I get inside, I find the room empty.

"I'm sure they'll be here," Olga says as she sets my plate of Syrniki with cheese and honey on top in front of me.

I give her a polite smile, but I know they're not coming.

"I don't like remembering that birthday because of how lonely it was. I hadn't seen Mama. I assumed she was in her bedroom. And although Papa was home, he spent the day in his office with the doors closed. Every time I went by and asked the guard if I could go in, he told me Papa was busy and couldn't see me."

"This seems to evoke more emotion than witnessing the violence."

"I never thought about it that way, but I guess you're right."

"There's nothing wrong with that." Masha tries to reassure me. "It's just an observation."

I nod and continue. "When it was time for dinner, I assumed I'd be eating alone. So, I was surprised when I walked into the dining room and saw Dimitri and Pyotr sitting at the table."

"There's our birthday girl." Dimitri gives me a big smile.

I sit across from the men who do their best to carry on a conversation with me. But neither of them is used to spending time with a girl, so we don't talk about more than the weather and how good Olga's cooking is. All through dinner, my eyes are drawn to the doorway, hoping to see Mama and Papa, but they never come.

After the meal, Olga emerges from the kitchen carrying a pink frosted cake with eleven candles.

"Don't light those yet," Dimitri says and makes a quick exit from the room. He returns a short time later with Mama and Papa, who apologize for running late.

Although everyone has smiles on their faces, I see beneath the masks to the pain they try to hide. After singing Pust' begut neuklyuzhe, I blow out my candles. Dimitri cuts the cake while Olga passes out the plates.

"Classes resume tomorrow," Papa says as we eat.

"Yes, they do." I'm looking forward to finally being able to leave the house.

"Pyotr will be accompanying you."

I drop my fork. "I don't want a guard at school."

"I did not ask if you wanted one," Papa says sternly. "You will have one."

"Fine."

"I must return to work." Papa stands. "S dnem rozhdeniya, moya babochka."

Mama walks out right after Papa, leaving me with Dimitri and Pyotr once again.

"Thank you for trying, Dimitri." I manage a small smile.

"They're doing the best they can right now."

"I know."

"That day marked twenty-one days that my sister was missing. I remember thinking Mama and Papa looked and sounded like the parents I knew, but that's where the comparison ended. No one was the same." I swipe at the stray tear that escapes and look at Masha. "I was scared and sad. I felt invisible."

Maxim (Ten Years Ago)

THE DOOR TO MY OFFICE FLIES OPEN, BANGING AGAINST the wall. "What the hell is wrong with you?"

"Did you forget what today is?"

"What are you talking about?" I'm annoyed by my nephew's unwelcome intrusion.

"It's Svetlana's birthday. The kids spent the entire day alone. Pyotr and I just had dinner with her, but what she needs is her parents."

How could I forget my daughter's birthday? "I will get Irina. We will be right there."

"I'll walk with you."

"I do not need a babysitter." Yet, Dimitri follows me anyway.

"Uncle Max, this has to stop. Your men are more than capable of carrying out this search on their own. You're neglecting—"

"Enough." I slice my hand through the air, stopping my nephew in his tracks. "I will not have you telling me how I should or should not conduct the search for my daughter. Do you hear me? Jelena is my daughter." I start walking away but stop and turn around quickly. "When you have walked in my shoes, you may tell me how to do my job. Until that time, keep your comments to yourself."

I take the steps two at a time, needing to put some distance between Dimitri and myself. When I get to our bedroom, I find Irina in the same position she has been in for weeks. She is lying on the bed with her back toward the door.

"Irina, I need you to get up." I grab her robe that is draped over the back of the armchair. "It is Svetlana's birthday."

"I can't go."

I sit next to my wife and stroke her forehead. "*Moya vozlyublenny,* we have both forgotten about Svetlana's special day. She is waiting to have cake with us."

Slowly, Irina pushes to a sitting position. Her complexion is pale from lying in this dark room for weeks. I offer my hand to help her stand and am alarmed when I notice the nightdress hanging off her shoulders from the weight she has lost. Now is not the time to bring that up. Instead, I help her into her robe and then take her hand as we go to the dining room.

We are gathered around the table to celebrate my Svetlana's eleventh birthday. It should be a day to celebrate the life of our special little girl. Looking around the table, I see it is not a celebration. My wife sits beside me, but her mind and heart are absent. Rather than Svetlana laughing with her sister, Dimitri and Pyotr are talking with Svetlana, trying to make this as normal as possible. And there is an empty chair where my Jelena should be sitting.

I attempt to interject myself into the conversation. "Classes resume tomorrow," I say.

"Yes, they do."

"Pyotr will be accompanying you."

She drops her fork. It clangs off her dish. "I don't want a guard at school."

"I did not ask if you wanted one. You will have one."

"Fine."

I believed my family was safe in our community. My girls were allowed to grow up and live normal lives. In a matter of minutes, that all changed. We can never go back to the way things were before.

There are new rules for my daughters. They will no longer be allowed off my property without a guard by their side. Jelena is my compliant, good-natured daughter. I know when I find her and bring her home, she will accept my directive with no argument. Svetlana, on the other hand, never misses the opportunity to challenge me. I knew she would fight me on this.

"I must return to work. *S dnem rozhdeniya, moya babochka.*" This is Svetlana's special day. I do not want to spoil it by arguing over insignificant details. Obviously, she is better off without me here right now.

Svetlana

I'M THANKFUL THAT TODAY'S SESSION IS OVER. Recalling the memories from that day was harder than I thought it would be. I really want to go back to my dorm and be alone, but I know my dorm mate, Mei, will be there. I spot Pyotr on his usual bench. When he sees me, he hurries over.

"Is everything okay?"

"That was a tough session. I need some time alone. Can I hang out in your room?" I won't be truly alone, but Pyotr's okay with silence.

"That's fine with me, but I should warn you, Slava's waiting for you outside."

"Did he say what he wants?"

"No."

I take a deep breath and walk outside. Slava's leaning against the building, his arms crossed over his chest. A small group of girls has gathered around him.

"Hi," I say, touching his arm and glaring at the now-silent girls. "Sorry, I'm late."

"Excuse me, please, ladies." Slava places his hand on my lower back and leads me away. "Don't tell me you're jealous?"

"Maybe." I shrug.

"There's no need. I came here for you, not them." His words tamper down the jealousy I'm feeling.

"I'm surprised to see you here. I thought you'd be back in St. Petersburg."

"I'm leaving tonight. I wanted to see you before I left. Can we talk?"

I'm exhausted physically and emotionally, but I can't say no to this man. "Sure. Is everything okay?"

"It is." He leads me to a concrete bench that's under a tree. "I enjoyed our time together this past weekend."

"Why does this sound like goodbye?"

"It isn't a goodbye." He lifts my chin, forcing me to look at him. "I'd like to see more of you."

"You would?" After I say the words, I realize how ridiculous I sound.

"I would," he chuckles. "If you're open to it, I'd like to discuss a contract."

"Um, sure."

"Are you okay, Lana? You don't seem like yourself."

"I had a long day. I'm just a bit tired."

"I'll email you a contract, but I want you to take your time to look it over. Get some rest before you make any decisions."

"I can do that."

"I do hope you say yes, though." He cups my cheek in his hand, and I hope he's going to kiss me. Instead, he says. "I have to go. I'll speak to you later in the week."

I watch as he walks away. Pyotr appears at my side just as Slava gets into his car. "Is everything okay?"

"Yeah, it is." He looks in Slava's direction and then back at me. He's opening his mouth to speak, but I cut him off. "Please, don't. I need one person in my corner."

"I'm always in your corner, little butterfly." Pyotr holds his hand out. "Come on, let's get back to the dorm for your alone time."

Pyotr keeps the lights off. "Go lay down and rest. I'll be here if you need me."

"Thanks." My head barely hits the pillow on his bed before I fall asleep and am thrust right back into my past.

"Are you excited to return to school today?" Pyotr asks.

"Yes." What was supposed to be a fun school holiday turned into a nightmare. Papa said I did everything, and I know he's been working non-stop to bring her home, but it hurts that both he and Mama are avoiding me. I'm sure they blame me for what happened.

I'm looking forward to returning to school where I know I'll have my friends. However, I'm not happy about having to bring a guard to school.

"I know you don't want me to go with you. I'll do my best to give you space."

"Thank you." Pyotr opens the front door for what I think is our walk to school.

"The car's warmed up already," he says proudly.

"The car?"

"Until your sister is found safe and the responsible people have been apprehended, your father is requiring me to drive you to and from school.

"Seriously?"

"I'm afraid so." Pyotr shrugs.

I want to scream and tell Pyotr there's no way I'm driving to school. I'm walking with my friends like Jelena and I used to do. But I know it won't do any good. Pyotr isn't in charge. He's not the one who made this stupid decision. He's always nice to me, so I don't want to give him a hard time. Instead, I get into the car and buckle my safety belt for the short ride to Krestovsky Preparatory Academy.

We drive past my friends, who are smiling and laughing as

they walk together. I sink down in my seat, hoping they don't see me being driven to school. A few minutes later, Pyotr turns into the school parking lot. I climb out of my father's gigantic vehicle, thankful we got there before my friends.

When we get inside the school's door, we're met by the director. "Welcome back, Svetlana," Director Valkov greets me. "And you must be the security Mr. Solonik advised us would be accompanying Svetlana?"

"Yes," Pyotr says, standing to his full height and crossing his arms over his chest.

Director Valkov lowers his voice as a group of students walk by. "I understand Mr. Solonik's reasoning, but I'm concerned your presence will upset the other children in Svetlana's classroom. I've set up a chair for you at the end of the hall."

"I will remain outside Svetlana's classroom door."

My eyes dart back and forth between the men. Pyotr's at least a foot taller than Director Valkov. And where the director is round and unfit, Pyotr has lots of muscle—Papa ensures all his guards exercise regularly.

"You must understand, I am tasked with ensuring the safety and security of all my students, not just Svet—."

"I have only one concern, Svetlana's safety. I will be outside her classroom. Unless you need Mr. Solonik to stop by?" Pyotr steps forward.

The hall fills with students who all avert their stares as they walk past the scene unfurling between the two men. I'm so embarrassed I want to crawl into a corner and hide.

"That won't be necessary," Director Valkov puts his hands up in surrender.

"Now, if there's nothing else, we will be on our way. I believe class is starting shortly."

"Yes, it is." He looks at me. "I hope you have a good first day back."

"Thank you," I say quietly.

Pyotr and I walk down the hall until we come to room number five.

"I'll be out here if you need anything." He offers me a kind smile.

"Okay." I take a deep breath and peek through the window of the door. My classmates chat amongst themselves while Ms. Orlova writes on the blackboard, preparing for the day's lesson. When I step into the classroom, everyone goes silent. Ms. Orlova gives me a tight smile but says nothing as I walk past her to the closet, where I hand my coat. All eyes follow me as I make my way to the table I share with my best friend, Sofya.

"How was your break?" I ask as I sit.

"It was fine."

"Do you want to work on our dance during free time?" Sofya and I have studied ballet at the same dance academy since we were three years old. This summer, we're finally old enough to audition for the summer intensive program for pointe students. We've been working very hard on our audition routine.

"I don't think so." She looks across the aisle to where Lavra, another classmate, sits before looking back at me. "Over the holiday recess, my parents enrolled me in a different dance school. Lavra and I are going to be working on our choreography together."

I glance at Lavra, who's whispering something to Nadia, her tablemate. Then, they both look at me and laugh.

"Oh." My fragile heart shatters.

Sofya and I have been best friends for as long as I can remember. Why is Sofya doing this? I'm just about to ask her when Ms. Orlova calls the class to order. I thought coming back to school would be a welcome respite from the loneliness I've felt at home. Instead, I find I'm just as alienated here. Rather than focusing on the morning's lessons, my mind wanders.

Jelena, I need you to be okay. I need you to come home.

I don't realize how much time has passed until the lunch bell rings, startling me. I slide my book into the drawer under the table and file out of the room with my classmates.

I need to talk to Sofya, but she's too far ahead of me in the food line to get her attention. As soon as I'm through, I hurry to the table where she's sitting. "Why did you change ballet schools?"

Lavra whispers something to Sofya, and she doesn't answer me.

"Can I sit here?"

"I'm not allowed to be friends with you anymore. I'm sorry," Sofya says quietly.

"You're not allowed to be friends with me anymore?" I don't understand what's going on.

"None of us want you here," Lavra interrupts. "There's a table over there." She points to a small table in the corner.

I wait, hoping Sofya says something, anything to make this better. But she doesn't. She just ignores me.

I drop my head and walk to the empty table in the corner of the cafeteria. After I sit, I look around the room at everyone else. They're all laughing and talking. I'm the only one alone. As hard as I try, I can't stop tears from escaping. I wipe my face quickly, not wanting the girls to see me cry. They don't need any more ammunition than they already have to hurt me.

Movement catches my eye. It's Pyotr, and he's hurrying in my direction. It's only seconds before he's at the table, pulling out the chair next to me. "What's wrong?"

"Nothing."

"I may not know a lot about children, but I do know they don't cry when there's nothing wrong."

"Everything's different." I swallow over the growing lump in my throat. "My parents don't speak to me anymore. I thought I'd at least have my friends at school, but they're gone now, too."

"It's your first day back. I'm sure everyone's just getting back into the routine of things."

"Sofya," I say, looking in her direction. "Was my best friend. Now, she won't speak to me, and neither will anyone else. Everyone hates me."

"That's not true."

"But it is." I swipe at the fresh wave of tears spilling down my cheeks. "I want to go home."

"Please don't cry," Pyotr says nervously as he searches the room. His gaze stops at the table where Sofya, Lavra, and several other girls point in our direction and laugh.

He wastes no time pulling out his cell phone and typing something. A few minutes later, his phone buzzes. After he reads whatever's on the screen, he turns to me. "Come on." He takes my hand.

"Where are we going?"

"Home."

Pyotr is summoned to Papa's office seconds after we walk into the house. Dimitri's already in there. The door is cracked open, so I sit against the wall with my knees pulled up to my chest, listening while they talk. I know I shouldn't be here, but I want to hear what's going on. I need to know what's going to happen next.

"I do not understand why you brought her home early," Papa says.

"I couldn't make her stay when it was clear she was being made fun of."

"And you gave him permission to bring her home?"

"I did," Dimitri answers confidently. "She's been through too much the past few weeks. There's no reason for her to endure any more cruelty."

"Svetlana knows to ignore such childish behavior. She is a young girl who needs to be in school."

"Maybe you can hire a tutor? At least until things calm down," Dimitri suggests.

Papa's heavy footsteps come closer, and I scramble to get up quickly and disappear.

"I know you are there, Svetlana." Papa's voice stops me in my tracks. "Come back here."

"Yes, sir."

"In." He points, and I step into his office.

"Pyotr and Dimitri." Papa glares at the men. "Feel you will be *better served by continuing your studies at home. So, until a quali-fied tutor is hired, Dimitri will be overseeing your lessons."*

"Thank you, Papa." I reach to hug him, and his cell rings.

He looks at the screen. "Go on, now. I must take this call."

Pyotr follows me to the door. "Everything will be okay, little butterfly."

I startle awake and sit straight up. I'm momentarily disoriented and rub my eyes. Slowly, the room comes into focus.

"You okay, little butterfly?" Pyotr asks from his seat across the room.

What he said earlier is true. No matter what's happened, he's always been in my corner, looking out for me.

Svetlana

WHEN I WOKE UP MONDAY, I HAD AN EMAIL WAITING for me.

> Svetlana,
> I enjoyed our time together this weekend and am looking forward to spending much more time together in the near future. I've written a contract that will serve our unique needs as a couple. Take your time reviewing everything. Don't hesitate to call or text me if you have any questions or changes you'd like to make. I'm really looking forward to embarking on this new adventure with you.
> ~Slava

I've read the contract several times and am pretty confident in my understanding. I don't broadcast being in the BDSM lifestyle because so many still find it a taboo subject. But this is one time that I wish I had let more people get close to me. I could really use someone to talk to about whatever is developing between Slava and me.

"Whatcha looking at?" Mei asks, and I quickly switch tabs.

"Just doing some last-minute research for an assignment."

"Are you still up to going out for dinner tonight?"

"Of course."

"No dates with that sexy guy?"

"What guy?"

"The guy who picked you up last weekend." She smirks. "You've been holding out on me."

"I really haven't. There's nothing—"

"You didn't come back to the dorm. There's much more than nothing," she says, interrupting me. "If I don't leave now, I'll be late for class. I expect to hear every detail tonight." Mei flits out the door before I can argue any further.

I pull the contract back up after Mei leaves. Slava texted me Monday to ensure I got his email, but I haven't heard from him since. He wanted to give me enough space to consider the contract without feeling any pressure from him.

Overall, I'm okay with everything he's proposed in the contract. Except for one thing—I'm not prepared to surrender all my time to a Dominant. Since I don't have class for another hour and I have some time alone, I send him a text.

Me: I'm done reading the contract.

Slava: Tell me your thoughts.

Me: I don't want to commit to anything during the week.

Slava: Can you explain why not?

Me: There are only a few weeks left in the school term. Final exams are coming up. I want to keep this to only a weekend arrangement.

Slava: I appreciate your honesty. I'd prefer more, but if weekends are all you'll commit to, I'm willing to accept that—for now.

Me: I also don't want to agree to anything that extends past the end of my school term.

Slava: I can agree to a short-term contract on one condition.

Me: What is that?

Slava: That you agree to revisit this conversation after school is out for the summer.

Me: Okay. Thank you for understanding.

Slava: That's what this stage is for.

Slava: Now that we're both on the same page. I'd like you to spend the weekend at the hotel with me.

Me: I think that can be arranged.

Slava: I'll text you when I'm in Moscow.

"I still wish you would've been the one to tell me about this weekend," Pyotr complains in the elevator on the way up to Slava's room. "I don't like getting a call from Slava and not knowing what the hell he's talking about."

"It honestly slipped my mind." I've been so busy this week that I didn't have a second to stop and think about the logistics of the weekend. Thankfully, Slava thought ahead and arranged for Pyotr to stay in the room next to ours.

After a long walk down the hall, we stop in front of room 4031. I raise my hand, but the door opens before I get the chance to knock. "You must have ESP or something," I laugh nervously.

"Nothing that fancy. Just a call from security letting me know you arrived on my floor." Slava glances over my shoulder. "Pyotr, good to see you again."

"Likewise," Pyotr answers stiffly.

"Come in." Slava grabs two keycards from the table inside the foyer of his suite. "For your room and mine."

Pyotr takes the offered cards. "Svetlana will keep her phone on at all times. If I text, she has ten minutes to respond, or I will be in."

"That's a bit much, don't you think?"

After spending the night with Slava last weekend, Pyotr has been very overprotective. I don't know what's going on with him, but I don't like it. "I'm a grown woman. I don't need to check in with you."

"That's your choice." He shrugs. "If you don't, I'll be in to check on you myself. And something tells me you don't want that to happen."

"I will ensure Lana's phone is on, and she responds to any messages you send."

My gaze snaps from Pyotr to Slava. "Are you kidding?" I snap.

"You may not have signed the contract yet, but you should watch your tone, *Moya nevinnyy malysh.*"

"I'm sorry."

"Go have a seat. I want to speak to Pyotr privately." Slava waits for me to follow his orders before he turns back to Pyotr. The men step just outside the door, and I'm unable to hear what they're saying. Several minutes later, Slava closes the door and joins me at the table. "Let's get this contract signed, shall we?"

"I like that idea."

"Please check it over one last time to ensure everything is as we discussed."

I skim the pages of the contract, not at all concerned about the accuracy. "It looks good. Do you have a pen?" We take turns signing both copies.

"I'm glad that's out of the way. Now, strip. There'll be no need for your clothes this weekend."

After seeing Slava's reaction when I undressed at the club, I wanted to try to elicit the same response a second time. Grabbing the hem of my shirt, I pull it over my head, exposing my breasts to him.

"I don't like knowing you're wearing nothing under your clothes when you're with other men." He crosses his arms across his chest.

I smile as I shimmy my leggings down and step out of them. "It's all with you in mind, Sir."

"Is it now?" The corner of his mouth turns up. "Get on all fours on the bed."

I climb onto the bed and look over my shoulder. He takes his time unbuttoning his white dress shirt. The outline of his erection is clear. It's empowering knowing I excite him. I grow wet with need as I watch him take off his shirt. Once again, he leaves his pants on, and I feel a tinge of disappointment.

"What's wrong?"

"Nothing."

His hand connects with my ass, and I let out a squeal. "That was the wrong answer. Let's try that again. "What's wrong?"

"I was hoping we were going to have sex tonight."

"Is that so?" His hand makes contact with my body again.

"Yes, Sir."

"And what makes you think we won't?"

"You're wearing your pants like last time."

He leans over my back. His erection presses against me. *"Moya nevinnyy malysh,* we're only just getting started."

His strikes come fast and hard. Each time his hand connects with my body, the repetitive thoughts that plague me on a daily basis begin to quiet until there's nothing left but silence. As my breathing slows, my body relaxes. The warmth of Slava's body near mine returns as his fingers slide inside my wet center.

"Does this feel good?" I nod. His fingers still, and I groan in frustration. "Let's try that again. Does this feel good?"

"Yes, Sir. Very good." He starts moving, and my body climbs to the edge of an orgasm. Just as I'm about to fall over the precipice, they're gone. I drop my head in frustration.

"Get on your back." In this position, I'm able to watch as Slava reaches into a black leather bag pulling out several bundles of red rope. "Curious?"

"Very."

"This is going to be a challenging position. I'll be checking in periodically to make sure you're okay. You are to use your safewords if you feel even the smallest thing wrong. Do you understand?"

"Yes, I do." The reason for his safety reminder becomes apparent immediately. Slava lifts my right leg, binding it to my outstretched right arm. I'm just about to ask where he's going to anchor the rope when he reaches behind the grey headboard attached to the wall, and I hear a click.

"I take it you are not aware this hotel caters to a certain crowd?" he asks as he ties the rope to the hidden anchor. "The rooms are all equipped with discreet features." He moves to my other side and secures my arm and leg in the same fashion. "Last thing." Slava holds up silver nipple clamps connected by a chain. "Have you ever tried these?"

"No."

"I'm looking forward to this even more." His dark eyes sparkle with delight as he places one of the clips over my erect nipple. He slides the ring down, making it tight. Slava makes quick work securing the second clamp and then gives a gentle tug. "Perfect."

Lust swirls in his gaze as he stands back and takes in my body, which is on full display. "Does everything feel okay?"

Slava was right. This is a challenging position. One I don't know that I'd be able to hold had it not been for years of ballet lessons that ensured my flexibility. The clamps make my nipples ache, but instead of being unpleasant, it's fueling my desire. "Yes, everything is good."

Seeming satisfied with my answer, Slava steps out of view. Lady Gaga's "I Like it Rough" begins to play a second before the lights dim. When he comes back into view, he unbuckles his belt and lowers his pants and boxers. My eyes stay glued on him as he fists his erection, pumping his hand up and down his hard length.

"Do you like watching?" The tone of his voice is low.

I'm unable to form words, so I nod.

"Tsk tsk." He shakes his head. "That won't do at all."

"Yes. I like watching."

"That's better," he says, positioning himself between my legs on the bed. "I will not be gentle." The words have barely left his mouth when he rams himself inside me. He sucks in a quick breath. "Fuck, Lana. All week I've been imagining this." He pulls out and enters me again fast and hard. There's no more conversation as he keeps up his punishing rhythm. It doesn't take long before I feel an explosion of sensation, and I cry as waves of pleasure crash over me. My body convulses from the intensity of my release.

"You look so sexy when you come. I want you to do it again."

He keeps one hand firmly on my bound leg, steadying himself as he drives into me. The other hand goes to work expertly, inching my body closer to another climax. His cock grows harder inside me, and I know he's close. "You're going to come with me. Ready?"

Slava's muscles tense and release as his body begins to pulse inside me. He grabs the chain and pulls the clamps off. The sudden rush of sensation causes an explosion of pleasure. I moan loudly as I drown in a sea of blissful sensations.

"Fuck, Svetlana. That was incredible." He drops his head as he catches his breath and withdraws from my body. A trail of liquid drips from me. His eyes narrow as he runs his fingers through our combined arousal, circling the tight ring of muscle. "Has anyone ever taken you here?"

"No, Sir."

"Before this weekend is over, I will have you there, too. I plan to own every part of your body."

Svetlana

THE REST OF THE WEEKEND IS SPENT WITH ME NAKED and bound in any number of positions. Pyotr keeps his promise and checks on me several times. Slava makes sure I'm able to text him right back. Pyotr knows I'm into BDSM, but the last thing I want is him coming in here and seeing it.

It's early Sunday morning. The sun is peeking up from the horizon when my phone vibrates. Slava is still asleep, his arms wrapped around my body. I move carefully, hoping not to wake him, and grab my phone.

Pyotr: What time are we leaving today?

Me: I don't know. Slava's still asleep.

"Is that your guard already?" Slava asks.

"I'm sorry. I didn't mean to wake you." I lay back down and turn to face him. Slava's thirty-five, nearly fifteen years older than me. But lying here with his dark hair messy from sleep, he looks young and carefree. "He wants to know what time we're leaving."

"We're not even out of bed yet."

Me: Later this afternoon. I'll get back to you as soon as I have a definite time.

"It'll be a long week until I see you again." Slava positions me so I'm straddling him." I plan to get my fill of you before we go. I want you up here." He pulls me toward his face.

In a moment of hesitancy, I resist. His mouth was on me more times than I can count this weekend, but I've never sat on a man's face.

"What is it?" he asks.

"I'm not sure. I've never."

"I won't force you, but I'd very much like it if you did."

I bite my lip, still uncertain. My decision is made when I look down and see the hunger in his eyes. I position myself so my pussy is in line with his mouth. He explores me with his mouth licking and sucking as he goes. Everything he's done until this point was incredible, but it doesn't compare to this right now. I'm already panting with need when he starts to fuck me with his tongue. Oh my God, the feeling is so intense in this position.

"Slava. I can't. I—" My body tenses up as pleasure radiates from my core and spreads through my body in a kaleidoscope of sensations. Every nerve ending in my body feels alive as wave after wave of ecstasy courses through me, and wetness gushes from my body. His tongue doesn't stop until the last contractions of my orgasm subside. My body is limp as he lifts me and lays me down beside him.

Slava props himself on his elbow. His face glistens with my arousal. "That's the perfect way to start a day." He tucks a strand of hair behind my ear. "I'm hopeful I'll have you in my bed every morning after your term ends."

"I need to get through these next few weeks before I can even think about break."

After breakfast and a quick shower, I again find myself at the mercy of Slava's endless desire. I'm currently bound in a spread-eagle fashion while he alternates exposing me to gentle and painful sensations.

I squeal when he drags an ice cube down my belly. My back arches as Slava uses his crop on my hardened nipples. He hasn't gone anywhere near my wet center, and I'm already close to climaxing. He reaches for something that's out of my sight. I hear a vibrator a second before feeling it on my clit. That small amount of contact is all it takes for me to orgasm again. My body has barely come down from the high when something cold presses against my other opening. Slava's been preparing me for this moment with his fingers and various toys.

"You need to relax, *moya nevinnyy malysh*."

I take a deep breath and do my best to relax the muscles. Gently, he slides the toy in and out until I feel it pass the initial tight ring of muscles. I tense at the sensation that borders on pain. This is the biggest butt plug he's used so far. Sensing my tension, he switches the vibrator back on, massaging my clitoris while gently rocking the toy back and forth until it's fully inside. I'm startled when the toy begins to vibrate. There are so many sensations happening at once. It's almost too much.

"Yellow."

Immediately, he turns the vibrators off. "Talk to me."

"There's so much happening at once," I say between breaths. "It's too much."

"Do you want me to stop?"

"No."

"Take a few deep breaths."

I close my eyes and concentrate on recentering myself. "I'm better. We can keep going."

Slava unties my arms and pushes the vibrator into my hand. "You're in charge of that now." He grins.

Pressing the button, the bullet springs back to life, and I begin pleasuring myself. My eyes close as I get lost in the arousal that's quickly building. Without warning, a dildo is slid inside. "Oh my God," I whisper. I'm stretched to a point where there's almost pain, but then he turns the dildo on, and the pain morphs into pleasure. My mind goes blank as I'm overcome with a torrent of sensation. I writhe beneath him as I ride waves of pleasure. When my orgasm finally stops, Slava makes quick work of untying my legs and removing the toys.

"Get on your hands and knees."

With shaky limbs, I comply with his demand and turn over. He positions himself behind me. I watch over my shoulder as he squirts some lube and penetrates me with his finger. Then, I feel his cock against me. I drop my head as he pushes against my entrance and breeches the muscles.

"I'll go slow," he says. "I don't want to hurt you."

I nod, and this time, he doesn't press for a verbal answer.

He pushes in a little further, and I gasp. Slava's hand comes around my body right to my clit. He plays with the oversensitive area, distracting me with pleasure as he fully sheathes himself inside me. "You're so tight." His voice is strained, and his body trembles. But then his self-control snaps. "Fuck, Lana. I can't be gentle." He grabs my hips as he pistons in and out. "I'm not going to last much longer."

His finger finds my clit once again, and he works me into a panting mess. I come calling his name. He follows me over the edge. Our bodies pulse in shared pleasure. My body collapses underneath him. Slava pulls out and gets off the bed. I roll over and watch the flex of his muscles as he walks into the bathroom. He comes back a few seconds later with a warm washcloth. Gently, he wipes me off before climbing into bed and pulling me close to him. I fall asleep listening to his whispers of how much he's enjoyed every second of his weekend with me.

"*Moya nevinnyy malysh*. It's time to wake up." He rubs my shoulder, and I slowly open my eyes. "I want to take a shower before we leave."

Slava sits up, throws his legs over the bed, and stands before turning around and offering me his hand. I follow him into the bathroom, admiring the flexing of his muscles as he walks in front of me. He adjusts the water and pulls me close to him under the hot stream. I know it's getting late, and he needs to leave, but the erection pressing against my belly gives away his need.

Lowering to my knees, I glance up at Slava as I open my mouth and take in his long, hard length. His dark eyes stay locked with mine as he allows me to set the pace. I've spent the weekend learning how he likes to be pleasured and use every lesson I've learned. I swirl my tongue around the head of his cock before dragging it through his slit, tasting his pre-cum. His hand tangles in my hair as I slowly and gently drag my teeth along his hard length.

As if he can't take it anymore, his hand flies out to brace himself against the tiled wall. With my hair wrapped around his other hand, he takes over. Slava isn't gentle as he fucks my mouth. Tears cascade down my face from the force of his cock hitting the back of my throat. His legs begin to tremble, and he comes inside my mouth. My eyes lock with his as ribbons of cum shoot down my throat, and I do my best to swallow everything he has to give. I feel powerful watching him come undone.

After he catches his breath, he helps me to my feet and then leans over to kiss me. It's the first time his lips have touched mine. Somehow, it feels more intimate than anything we've done so far. "You're making it very hard for me to leave you." He watches me, seeming to gauge my response.

"Then, I've done my job well."

The sun is beginning to set as we leave the hotel. Pyotr follows a short distance behind. Slava walks me to our car and cages me in his arms. "I'll talk to you later in the week."

"Have a safe trip home."

Slava's lips meet mine for a gentle kiss before he turns and walks away. I watch until he drives away. As soon as he's gone, I get into the car and wait for Pyotr to join me.

"I thought you were only in a contractual relationship with Slava," he says as he gets into the driver's seat.

"That's all it is."

Pyotr chuckles. "Someone better tell him that because that guy has it bad for you."

The drive back to campus is quiet. Pyotr's observation caught me off guard, and I'm lost in my thoughts. Slava can't fall for me. Pyotr must be mistaken. All that's between us is a Dom/sub relationship. We have great chemistry in bed, but it's just sex. There are no feelings or emotions involved. He knows I can't commit to anything beyond the next few weeks.

Svetlana

I SLEPT THROUGH MY ALARM THIS MORNING. IT'S A good thing Pyotr was there and woke me up, or I probably would've slept straight through classes today. I'm going to have to start working out more to keep up with Slava's stamina because I'm wiped after this weekend's sexathon. Finally, my last class is over. I don't know how I made it through the day. I'm supposed to have an appointment with Masha, but I don't feel up to it today.

I have to walk past her office to get to Pyotr, who's sitting in his usual spot. It must be my lucky day because her door is still closed. Picking up my pace, I walk past her office with the intention of getting to Pyotr and getting out of here.

I'm almost in the clear when the door opens, and Masha steps out. "I apologize for running late. There was an emergency I had to attend to."

"It's not a problem."

"Come on in."

I look between her door and my guard at the end of the hall. "I need to give my bag to Pyotr first."

"You always bring your bag with you. Is everything ok?" I

don't know the correct answer, so I say nothing. "Svetlana." Misha touches my arm. "Coming to therapy is voluntary. If you don't want to have a session today, that's your choice."

"I was going to skip." I don't have any fight in me, so I give up and walk into her office. "I don't have a good reason other than I'm extra tired today."

"I remember my university days. The last few weeks of the term are always stressful." She smiles kindly.

"There's just a lot going on right now." I flop onto her couch.

"I get the feeling this is about more than just school."

I drop my head back and groan. "I thought I knew what I wanted, but now I'm not so sure."

"We can talk whatever this is through if you'd like."

"Papa and Mama don't know that I changed my major yet."

"I thought you were going to tell him over the holiday break?"

"So did I. But it was the anniversary of my sister's abduction, and everyone's emotions were running high. I didn't want to make things worse."

"That's understandable." She taps her pencil against her chin. "Something tells me that isn't the only thing bothering you."

"Did anyone ever tell you that you're very perceptive?" I chuckle.

"That's what they pay me the big bucks for." Masha smiles.

"I guess now's as good of a time as any to tell you. I applied to New York University in the United States and was accepted."

"Congratulations. That sounds exciting."

"I've wanted this for so long. It's a chance to be on my own in a place where no one knows my family or me. Do you know what I mean?"

"I do." She jots something down in her notebook before looking back up at me. "What has you second-guessing your decision?"

"Remember I told you I bumped into someone I knew back home?"

"Yes."

"He comes to Moscow every week for business. We've been spending time together while he's here." I pull my feet under my legs. "It was just supposed to be something fun to do on the weekend. And it has been. What I didn't count on was falling for him."

"And now you're questioning your decision to go to the United States for school."

"Exactly. What should I do?"

Masha laughs. "You know better than that. This isn't about what *I* think you should do. I'm here to help you sort through your thoughts and feelings and to help you look at things from every angle. But in the end, this is your life, and only you're in charge of what decision you eventually come to."

"I wish that were true."

"One of the most important parts of taking charge of your life is communication. You need to voice your plans and your concerns with the people that'll be affected."

"Dimitri used to tell me the same thing, but it's the part I've always struggled with."

I don't know what Papa was thinking, assigning Dimitri to oversee my education. It turns out he makes a good teacher, with the exception of all his supposed-to-be funny computer jokes. He's actually pretty smart and makes my lessons interesting. As a bonus class, he's been teaching me some basic computer hacking skills—something I swore I wouldn't tell Papa about.

Unfortunately, Dimitri's leaving tomorrow. He's going back to Ukraine, where he lives with his mom. He wants to spend the last few weeks with her before he has to serve his conscription.

"I wish I could go with you."

Dimitri chuckles. "You realize I live in a village that could probably fit inside your house, right?"

"At least no one would know I was a coward that ran when—"

"Woah," he interrupts. "You are not a coward. I don't want to hear you speak that way, ever. Do you understand?"

I look down and make no move to answer. Dimitri puts his

finger under my chin, lifting my face to look at him. "First, you're a young girl. There was no way you could've fought two grown men. Instead, you did something just as important. You paid attention and gave us details we'd never have been able to get. If not for you, your father wouldn't have had any leads. We wouldn't have known where to start looking."

"Little good it did. Jelena's still missing, and it's my fault."

"Lana, what happened was not your responsibility."

"Then why do my parents hate me?"

"They don't hate you." He closes the textbook we were working in and shifts to look at me. "I know things have been different around here. Your papa is doing everything he can to find Jelena. You have to try to understand how difficult this is for him. Every day that goes by makes him feel even more helpless. He's channeling all his fear and anger into his search. He barely stops to eat or sleep. And your mama is struggling with grief in her own way. They're doing their best to get through this nightmare one minute at a time. But they don't hate you. You'll see, as soon as your papa finds Jelena, everything will return to normal."

"I don't think that's true. They're always going to blame me, hate me for what happened."

"Have you considered talking to them?"

"How? Mama doesn't leave her bedroom, and Papa's always working. I used to be able to go into his office to see him, but not anymore. No one will let me in. I know he's looking for Jelena, and that's important. I don't want to take him away from that, but—I don't know." My voice trails off.

"Your parents haven't stopped loving you. I know this is all really hard, but you need to tell them how you're feeling."

"I didn't take Dimitri's advice."

"I'm sensing a pattern.

"Communication was never my strong suit." I shrug. "Dimitri left a few weeks later. He was the only person spending any real time with me, so that was a tough goodbye. What was even worse was the next tutor Papa hired." I let out a small laugh.

In Dimitri's place is this bowtie-wearing guy, Sergei, who calls himself a teacher. Listening to him teach is as dull as watching American football.

I immediately decide I don't like him and make it my mission to give him a hard time—something that's not difficult to do. So far, I've tested this theory with pen clicking, doodling instead of taking notes, playing the different ringtones at the highest volume, and slipping my preferred reading behind my assigned reading. What really aggravates Sergei the most is cracking my chewing gum.

He's so predictable it's not even a challenge. I misbehave, he lectures me on expected behavior. I roll my eyes, and he answers with a ridiculous, frustrated grunt and a threat to tell Papa. I ignore him and continue whatever I was doing in the first place. We play this game of cat and mouse until three o'clock when I'm released from the torture called education.

Today, Sergei is lecturing on Russian history. I stifle a yawn, wishing Dimitri were still here. He made even the most dreadful subjects feel less like splitting frog hair three ways and more like something I actually wanted to listen to.

"Svetlana, you must pay attention," Sergei reprimands for the millionth time.

"I'm listening."

"What did I just say?"

I scan the textbook in front of me, trying to come up with an answer.

"I haven't been on that page for the past fifteen minutes." He sighs loudly. "Your grades are beginning to suffer because of your childish behavior. I'm left with no other choice than to report your deficient progress to Mr. Solonik."

"Whatever." I shrug.

Sergei darts to Papa's office every day after school to give his daily report on my negative behavior. I don't know why he thinks I'll suddenly start caring about it now. I stopped caring about everything and everyone.

"Can you tell me more about why you stopped caring?"

"At that point, I was convinced my parents had all but forgotten about me. I guess I figured if I didn't care, didn't let anyone close to me, that I'd be protecting myself from getting hurt again." I shrug.

"How did that work for you?"

"Before *that* day, my life was perfect. At least, that's what I thought. I had a lot of friends to play with and my sister to talk to. I went to my ballet lessons, which I loved. And I had my parents. I was close to both of them, but especially my papa." Tears prick the back of my eyes. "In an instant, everything changed. My life was unrecognizable. I no longer had friends, ballet, or my parents. That's when I decided to put up walls. I could smile and pretend, but I refused to let anyone get close to me."

"Unfortunately, your family's reaction to a significant trauma is not uncommon. Everyone processes these events in their own way. Oftentimes, without outside support, people tend to struggle in the aftermath."

"Svetlana." Masha waves her hand, getting my attention.

"I'm sorry. Can you repeat what you said?"

"You've done a great job today, but clearly, you're exhausted. Why don't we end it here for today?" Masha closes her notebook and rounds her desk.

"I think that's a good idea." I stifle a yawn.

"I'd like you to do something for me this week."

"Okay," I say hesitantly. Masha's never given me homework.

"I want you to tell your ten-year-old self that none of this was her fault. You've carried so much guilt over your sister's abduction. It's time to let that go. Whether you write a letter or look in a mirror and say it, I'd like you to tell her she's not to blame for anything that happened. Can you do that?"

"I'll try."

It's raining as we walk back to my dorm. Both Pyotr and I are soaked by the time we make it to the building. When I get to my room, I change into dry clothes and prepare to do my homework.

As hard as I try, I can't focus. All I can hear is Masha telling me I need to stop blaming myself for Jelena's kidnapping.

The problem is, I don't think I can do that. All these years later, I still replay that day in my head over and over again, trying to figure out what I could've done differently so that my sister would still be here today.

Maxim (Ten years ago)

"I feel Svetlana would be better served enrolled in a more traditional school setting," Sergei drones on.

Every day after Svetlana's lessons conclude, it is the same story. Sergei stands in my office, wasting my time. Precious minutes better spent searching for Jelena, with his constant complaints about my daughter's inattention and negative behaviors.

"Perhaps you do not know how to properly engage a student." I raise an eyebrow.

"I assure you I'm a skilled educator. The problem is Svetlana. Your daughter is—"

I jump from my chair, nearly knocking it over. My sudden movement draws the attention of my guards. "Be very careful with your next words, Mr. Barkov."

He stands in an apparent challenge. "When I was offered this position, I was led to believe your daughter was an advanced student with pristine manners. It has been my experience that she's nothing more than a spoiled brat."

I grab the man by his collar. "What did you say?"

"Your daughter is a sp—"

I cock my fist back, but Pyotr and Timur jump in, saving this pathetic excuse of a man from the recourse he has earned.

"Get this *mudak* out of my house. If I ever see his face again—"

"I've got it, boss." Timur grabs the man by his arm. "Let's go."

"Svetlana would never act that way. He clearly has no idea how to engage and teach a student." I pace back and forth in front of the floor-to-ceiling window that overlooks my property. Behind me, Pyotr clears his throat, and I spin around. "Is there something you want to add?"

"May I speak openly without fear of retaliation?"

Although I have reached the end of my patience today, I nod, giving my trusted guard permission to speak.

"Since Jelena's kidnapping, life has changed drastically for everyone. You've been searching twenty-four hours a day, which has made you unavailable to your family. Mrs. Solonik is held up in her room, losing herself deeper and deeper into depression." He takes a step closer, a brazen move, given my current temperament. "I have no children, so I can't say I would handle things differently. Svetlana is only a little girl. One who was at her sister's side when she was abducted. Arguably, she's endured the most trauma."

"If she needs something, she'll come to one of us. Svetlana knows we are here for her."

"Does she?"

Pyotr's veiled accusations are irritating me. "Of course," I snap.

"I may be overstepping, but I'm asking you to think about it for a minute. Mrs. Solonik used to spend a great deal of time with the girls. Right now, she's struggling to get through each day. Lana used to be free to come and go in your office, but now your door is always closed. I've been out there when the guards turn her away. The look on her face breaks my heart." He pauses, closing his eyes for a moment.

"Then there was school. It may have only been one day, but I saw what she went through. Rather than finding support from her friends, she was ridiculed. Svetlana's scared and sad. Worst of all, she's alone. Her behavior with Sergei is a desperate attempt to get attention from her parents."

Pyotr eyes me cautiously as I sink into the armchair by my desk. I lean forward, holding my head in my hands. His words are heavy and difficult to hear. My nerves have been on a hairpin trigger. Jelena has been gone for eight and a half weeks. With each day that passes, I know my chances of finding my daughter unharmed dwindle.

I have failed to see that my family is falling apart right before my eyes. The Dominant/submissive dynamic Irina and I share came to a sudden stop the moment we learned of Jelena's disappearance. I neglected to care for my submissive, my wife. I am certain the very foundation of our relationship is on unsure footing.

And my dear Svetlana. The day Jelena was taken, I was in awe of her composure as she relayed those critical details to us. All I saw was her bravery. I have not stopped long enough to consider that she is living through this in the same way as her mama and me. As Pyotr pointed out, she is possibly more affected because she watched her sister be dragged away.

"My God, what have I done? Where do I start? How do I fix this mess?"

"Svetlana's in her room. Go talk to her," Pyotr says quietly. "We'll continue working here. If we get any important information, I'll make sure it gets to you immediately."

"I will have my cell on me at all times." I walk to the door and stop to look back. "Thank you." Pyotr nods.

"Svetlana." I knock. "May I come in?"

Her door flies open. "Did you find her?"

"No, I have not."

"Oh." She drops her head and climbs onto her bed, sitting with her legs crossed.

I sit next to her. "Sergei paid me a visit earlier."

"I figured." She shrugs.

"Is there anything you would like to say about your behavior?"

"Not really." She picks up a book that's on her bedside table.

She knows this kind of flippant attitude is unacceptable. I try to remain patient. "Svetlana, we need to talk." I soften my voice. "About Jelena."

Her head shoots up. "What about Jelena?"

I take the book from her hands and set it aside. "Finding your sister and bringing her home has been my top priority—"

"Did Gavriil tell you where she is yet?" My face must give away my shock at hearing her question because she continues, "I know your men brought him here."

My body tenses. "Who told you that?"

My girls know I am in the Bratva and that my job is dangerous. It is something I have never hidden from them. However, they are children, and I work hard to ensure their lives are not affected by what I do. Whichever one of my guards told her about this is a dead man.

"No one. I was in the kitchen with Olga a few weeks ago when Misha and a few of the other guards pulled up. They dragged Gavriil from the backseat. I don't know what happened after that because Olga made me leave."

I must remember to thank Olga. After Misha and the other men finished questioning Gavriil, I had him brought to a holding cell near the guards' housing on my property. Ordinarily, we would have disposed of him right away, but we hoped that, with continued pressure, Gavriil would give us more information. I did not realize Olga had Lana in the kitchen. Gavriil was not in good shape when I left him. Seeing that could only have added more trauma to what she was already dealing with. I cannot imagine the trauma Svetlana has been living with after seeing him.

"Why did you not say anything before now?"

"I've tried to come to your office to see you, but you're always too busy and can't see me."

"I am never too busy to see you. The guards will be informed that you are not to be turned away." She nods. "And I am sorry you had to see that."

"It didn't bother me. Did he tell you who took Jelena and where she is?"

"That is not for you to worry about."

"Why not?" She sits taller, signaling she's ready to dig her heels in and fight.

"Because you are a little girl who should not be involved in my business."

"I'm not a little girl. I'm eleven years old, and I was the one holding Jelena's hand when they took her. I think I've earned the right to ask for some answers."

I study her, considering what she's said. What I see, or rather what I do not, surprises me. There is no trace of the carefree child who was writing letters to Ded Moroz. Whether I like it or not, she has lost the innocence of childhood. And she is right. She deserves answers. "Yes, he gave us some names."

"But you haven't found them yet?"

"No. I have not."

"Did you kill Gavriil?"

I do not want to, but I must answer her honestly. After we arrived home from Serbia, I paid him a final visit. It was clear we had gotten all the information from him. His life was worthless to me, and I took it. I fear she will never look at me the same way once she knows I am a killer. "Yes. I did."

"Are you going to kill me too?"

"Why would you say something like that?"

"Gavriil was responsible for setting up Jelena's kidnapping. He told you the information you needed, and then you killed him." She stands and faces me. "Jelena wanted me to hurry, and I gave her a hard time. When the men were dragging her away, I didn't fight hard enough, and then I ran away. I gave you the information you needed to find Gavriil. So, however, you wish to punish me. If you want to kill me—"

"Stop," I say, raising my voice. Then, I take her hand in mine. "What would make you think I could ever kill you?"

"After I told you everything I remembered, you sent me away. Since then, I'm not allowed to come into your office to see you. If I was stronger or hadn't run away, Jelena would still be here."

"You did exactly what you were supposed to do. If you had not run, they might have taken you too."

"I didn't tell you that the man who smelled like vodka grabbed me."

My heart skips a beat. "What do you mean?"

"He grabbed me. He was going to take me too, but the man holding Jelena told him to let me go and that they didn't want me." A tear slips from her pretty blue eyes. "Why did they want to take Jelena?"

"That is not something for you to worry about."

"Papa." She puts her hands on her hips. "I need to know, please."

I hate that Svetlana has been exposed to evil at such a tender age. I cannot lie or pretend it does not exist. "Gavriil's father, Rudolf, deals in humans. He steals and sells them for large sums of money. He used Gavriil to win Jelena's affection. Then, he waited for the perfect opportunity to get back at me."

"What did he get back at you for?"

"About a year ago, I found out about a shipment of humans coming through St. Petersburg. Rudolf thought I would look the other way, but I did not. I alerted my contact in the *politsiya*. Several of his top men went to prison for a very long time."

She nods, and a small smile appears on her face. "I knew you're one of the good guys. But, Papa, I still don't understand why they didn't take me too."

"I do not have that answer. But I am grateful. My heart would not be able to handle it if you were both taken."

"So, you don't hate me?"

"I could never hate you, *moya babochka*. I am sorry your mama and I have been blinded by our suffering. We failed to see how much you are hurting, too." I open my arms, and she falls into my embrace. Everything my child has been holding in rushes to the surface, and the floodgates open. Sobs wrack her little body. My heart breaks with the realization of just how badly Svetlana's been hurting. Because of my negligence, she has been hurting alone. "Let it all out, *moya babochka*. I am here. You are not alone anymore." When the intensity of her grief subsides, I hold her back so I can see her face. "Things will be different from now on."

That is a promise I refuse to break. I must get my house in order.

Maxim (Ten years ago)

THE SEARCH FOR JELENA CONTINUES. DESPITE HAVING resources and connections around the world, we have not found her yet. I have never felt more helpless. That is why I threw myself into micromanaging every step of this search. Instead, I should have been relying on the men I not only employ but trust to continue working while I tended to my wife and daughter's needs. After holding Svetlana as she cried in my arms the other night, I knew I had failed my family and must do everything in my power to make things right.

I promised Svetlana things would change and have been doing my best to make that happen. Unfortunately, Irina is not in the same place as me, but I coerced her out of the bedroom for several meals. Although she was there physically, she merely picked at her food and did not engage in conversation.

Just a few months ago, my wife was full of life. Since Jelena's abduction, Irina has retreated inside herself. She has chosen to shut out the world. I cannot criticize her because I also did not handle this trial in a healthy manner. But Irina is strong. She is a fighter. She has just lost her way. Today, however, my wife will become reacquainted with her inner strength.

Despite the fact that it is mid-afternoon, our bedroom is

drenched in darkness. Irina is lying on her side, facing away from me. With sure steps, I walk to the windows and pull open the heavy drapes, allowing the bright sunshine to fill the room.

"It is time to get up." I allow time for Irina to respond, but she does not. "You have been in here long enough. I need you to get up."

"Go away." She closes her eyes in an attempt to shut me out.

Before this, Irina would never have shown such disrespect. My actions, as of late, have not earned her respect, so I cannot be angry. Instead, I sit next to her on the bed. "I know how much you are hurting because I am, too. But we cannot continue like this. We must do better for each other and for our girls."

"I can't, Maxim." Her voice cracks.

"You can."

"Please. Just leave me be."

I stand but not to leave. "*Moya vozlyublenny*," I say with authority, getting her attention. "You will get up now."

"Yes, *Gospodin*." Her voice is no more than a whisper. Slowly, she pushes to a sitting position and then to her feet. Her head lowered in respect.

I cup her cheek in my palm. "It is time for you to rejoin those who are living. Go and shower. We will be having dinner with Svetlana tonight."

She opens her mouth to argue, but I put my finger to her lips, silencing her. "I was blinded by my own fear and sorrow. I allowed not only our marriage but also our dynamic to suffer. For that, I am sorry." My finger traces the silver chain that threads through a diamond infinity symbol. "I ask that you allow me to retake my place as your Dominant."

"I would never deny you that place in my life." Tears fill her gray eyes. "I'm sorry I haven't been stronger. That I—"

"Shh." I pull her to me. "There is nothing to apologize for. We are both going to do better starting now."

Over the next few weeks, we begin to resemble a family again. Svetlana is excelling with her new female tutor. She has also returned to her ballet lessons, this time without an argument about being escorted by Pyotr. Irina has returned to her medical practice with a part-time schedule. And I am still working hard to find Jelena.

This evening, we are enjoying a quiet dinner together. "Irina, I need you to pack me a bag after dinner."

"Where are you going, Papa?"

Between the team I left with Radovanović in Serbia and the men here, we have been using every resource at our disposal to track down Valery and Boris. It has been trying on all of us.

After the pair departed from Serbia, they seemed to vanish without a trace. But finally, last week, we got a break. There was a hit on facial recognition from a bus station in Madrid. The two have altered their appearances and are traveling under new identities. The more concerning development is that Jelena was not seen with them.

I immediately called Nicholai Federov, a Russian transplant and colleague, to ask for his aid. It did not take more than an hour before he returned my call with information that the men had been successfully apprehended. After losing a few body parts, they told Federov Jelena was sold into a well-known trafficking ring in Patras, Greece.

I wanted to fly right out, but calmer heads prevailed, reminding me that my movements are most certainly being tracked. The last thing I want to do is jeopardize any element of surprise we have. The stakes are higher than ever. We must get there before Jelena's moved, again. So, after a tense conversation with Federov, I agreed to wait until a plan was implemented.

As of two days ago, my team was working remotely with a

smaller organized crime affiliate in Patras. The group was more than happy with our offer of key information in exchange for their help locating Jelena. Our new colleagues have been trying to bust this ring for several years. The information we traded gave them the leg up they had been waiting for.

We have learned that this trafficking ring is known for buying people and using them for prostitution. I cannot think about what that means for Jelena. The only thing I am able to focus on is getting her back. And I intend to be there when we do.

I will fly to Madrid in the morning and meet up with Federov. To anyone watching, it will appear that I believe Jelena is still in Spain. From there, Federov arranged a private flight to take me to Greece unnoticed. We could blow the entire plan with one wrong move on our part. Waiting this out is one of the hardest things I have done.

"I am going to Greece."

"Have you found her?" Irina asks.

"We are very close. I am confident this nightmare will be over within a few days."

"When do you leave?"

"First thing in the morning."

Maxim (Ten years ago)

Irina is asleep beside me. From spending several weeks primarily in bed, she still tires easily. But I have laid awake for hours. My mind is racing, imagining every scenario we may encounter in Greece. The sun is beginning to rise when my cell vibrates on the bedside table, startling me.

Pyotr: They're on the move.

Me: I am on my way down.

I intended to be with my men and rescue her myself, but receiving this text means they've located Jelena. They were instructed that if the opportunity presented itself, they should not hesitate. The important part is that Jelena is rescued as quickly as possible. Knowing this was a possibility, I ensured each man was equipped with body cams. If I am not there, I want to be sure I can look into the eyes of the scum who stole my daughter before their time on this earth comes to an end.

I slide out of bed, careful to not wake Irina. After getting dressed, I hurry down to the command center. I want to see my daughter as soon as possible. The hall outside the room is teeming with activity. When the men see me coming, they move out of the way, allowing me clear passage into the room. Misha, Timur, and Pyotr are gathered around the monitors.

"What's going on?" The images are grainy and too dark. "Where are they?"

"Morocco," Misha answers without taking his eyes from the screen.

His answer confuses me. "Why are they not in Greece?" I ask as I take a seat beside him.

"Early yesterday, we received intel that an auction site was located in Patras. Somehow, the group kept it running right under our noses." I watch him, waiting for more information. He takes a deep breath before answering, "As soon as Federov found out, he sent a team in, but the traffickers had already moved. They left behind two lowlifes who were more than eager to talk." He pinches the bridge of his nose. "Several weeks ago, Jelena was in the auction and was sold to a Moroccan named Farouk El Alami."

While Misha talks, my eyes are now glued to the screen. The men are getting into place outside a large mansion. "Are you sure the information was correct?" I need him to say there was a mistake.

"Yes, sir. There's no doubt."

Our conversation is interrupted by the sounds of gunshots and explosions. I watch in silent horror, waiting anxiously for the first glimpse of my daughter in the protective custody of my men. The wait feels like an eternity. My heart hammers in my chest, threatening to burst through my ribcage.

Without warning, the cameras go black.

"What the hell is going on?" I slam my fists on the table. "Get the cameras back online."

Pyotr and Misha's phones simultaneously buzz with incoming messages. "I'm trying, boss," Misha says as he types furiously. No image appears.

"Maxim," Pyotr says, putting his hand on my shoulder. "Our men turned their body cams off."

"Why?" Misha checks his phone and exchanges a worried look with Pyotr. "Somebody better say something. Where is Jelena? I want to see my daughter."

"They found Jelena's body," Pyotr says quietly.

"Give me the damn phone." I spring to my feet, and the chair scrapes loudly against the floor. "I demand to know why the fuck they would say something like that. They cannot make a correct identification. I should have hired a more qualified team. They will regret—"

"There's no mistake, boss."

As if a switch flips, my body transitions into work mode, and I question Misha like I would for any job. "When?"

"A few hours at the most."

"How?"

"Max," Misha says quietly. "You don't want to go there."

"Jelena is my daughter." My fist goes to my chest. "I want to know how the bastard killed her."

Killed her.

She is dead.

My daughter is dead.

My heart sinks into the pit of my stomach, and I struggle to comprehend the reality of the situation. I double over, gasping for my next breath.

Pyotr takes my arm. "Sit down, boss."

My world has been thrown off its axis. My precious daughter has been taken from me in the cruelest and most senseless way imaginable. A wave of guilt and anger washes over me. "Get out of my way," I roar, pushing him aside and hurrying out of the room. I stand in the middle of the hall as the crushing weight of sorrow threatens to consume me. I want to scream, to lash out at the world. Anything to bring my Jelena back. I'm lost in a haze of pain and confusion, unable to think or feel anything aside from an all-consuming sorrow.

I hear a man's voice, but I cannot make out what he is saying. My eyes attempt to blink open, but it takes several minutes for the room to come into focus and for me to recognize where I am—my office. I have no memory of how I got here.

"Boss." Misha's voice cuts through the thick haze.

"What?"

"Irina's asking to see you."

The pain in my heart is unbearable, like a sharp knife twisting inside me. I need to find some way to dull it. I snatch the bottle of vodka from the desk, my lips already anticipating the numbing effect of the alcohol.

"You've had enough." Misha rips the bottle from my hand.

"I am not a fucking child." My words slur together as I swipe at the bottle he holds just out of my reach. "Give it back."

"It's time to sober up." He pushes a plate of food closer to me. "You're going to eat, and then you need a shower. Irina and Svetlana are going to need you."

"I may be drunk." I poke my finger at my chest. "But I am still the one in charge here."

"Then sober up and fucking act like it." Misha's words are harsh.

A fresh wave of pain crashes over me, overwhelming and suffocating. I wish it would drag me under and end this unbearable agony. I whisper the words, barely able to accept they're real. "It was not a nightmare. She is really gone?"

"I wish it wasn't real." Misha's voice cracks. "Jelena's really gone."

I am Maxim Solonik, a *Pakhan*. I do not succumb to weakness or emotion.

Even as I tell myself that, tears spill from my eyes. "How do I tell my wife I did not arrive in time? That our beautiful daughter is dead."

I do not know if I am strong enough to do this.

Svetlana

THIS WEEK I HAVE THE DORM ROOM TO MYSELF SINCE
Mei is away on a university-sponsored trip with the education
department. I'm thankful my roommate is easy to get along with
and understanding about my guard living in the room next door.
Still, I'm also relieved she's away.

Usually, I'd cut classes and, with Pyotr's help, disappear for
the week. He's always a knowing accomplice to my avoidance
behaviors. However, this year, I'm not able to escape. There's a
mandatory three-day conference on campus—something I'm not
looking forward to. The only silver lining is all my other classes
have been canceled.

I hate this week. I hate the painful memories that always
come up.

Ten years.

This week marks ten very long years since the day I learned my
sister had become my guardian angel.

*Pyotr and I are in the library playing chess. There's constant
activity in the hall outside the room.*

"What's going on?"

"Nothing."

"That's not true. I know Papa didn't leave today. Do you know why?"

"Please don't give me a hard time. Just take your turn."

"Whatever." I roll my eyes. My hand is on the rook when Mama's blood-curdling wail fills every corner of the room. I jump up and rush to the door, but Pyotr's faster. He grabs me around my waist.

"You need to stay here."

"What's going on? Mama. Papa," I scream.

Pyotr's grip tightens. "Lana, please. Calm down."

Despite my best efforts to break free, I'm no match for his size or strength. My kicks and punches have no effect. He easily keeps his hold on me.

Misha appears in the doorway. "The boss said to let her go to him."

Pyotr lets go of me, and I take off down the hall to Papa's office. My feet skid to a stop when I see Papa on the floor, his arms around Mama, who's sobbing uncontrollably.

"No," I whisper.

"Moya babuchka," Papa looks up at me with red-rimmed eyes.

"Please, Papa." I take a step back. If he doesn't say it, then it can't be true. "Don't say it."

"I am sorry, Lana. I did not get there in time. I am so sorry."

My Papa is crying. "Stop." I cover my ears, shaking my head.

"Come here." Papa holds out his free hand. "Lana, please."

"No," I scream and bolt from the office toward the front door.

Barefoot and without a second thought, I throw it open and charge down the steps.

"Lana, come back," Pyotr yells from behind me.

My breaths come out in ragged gasps as my legs carry me further and further away. My lungs burn from the exertion, but the physical pain is nothing compared to the emotional turmoil. I can't stop running because that means facing the reality of what had just happened. And I'm not ready for that yet.

As I make my way into the wooded area behind our property, memories flood my mind. Happier times of running and playing here with Jelena. I spot our tree house in the distance and make a beeline for it. Climbing up the rickety ladder, I scurry across the floor, not caring if I get slivers from the old wood. Huddled in the corner, I pull my legs up to my chest and let the tears fall.

A few minutes later, Pyotr's head pokes from the entrance in the floor. "May I come in?"

I don't answer him. With a slight groan, he enters the small space and sits beside me as he tries to catch his breath.

"Jelena's dead, isn't she?"

"Yes."

"Who killed her?"

"A man named Farouk El Alami." Pyotr doesn't give me a hard time answering my questions.

"Is he dead?"

"Yes."

I look up at Pyotr. "Did Papa make sure he suffered before he died?"

"He did, yes."

"Good. I don't feel bad knowing Papa made sure that man was hurt before he had him killed. Does that make me a terrible person?"

"I don't think it does."

The cold coming through the open windows of the treehouse made me shiver uncontrollably. Pyotr takes off his heavy sweatshirt and passes it to me. I pull it over my head, thankful it's big enough to cover my legs, too. We sit in silence as snow begins to fall outside. Pyotr doesn't push me to talk, which I appreciate. Instead, we sit there, lost in our own thoughts.

I can't escape the memory of Jelena's hand. How it felt as it slipped from mine. I clutch Pyotr's sweatshirt tighter as my body begins to shake harder. "I held onto her as tight as I could. I tried not to let go, but they were so much stronger than me," I mutter between sobs. "I'm a coward." The tears fall harder. I can't control my body as I begin to retch violently. It's painful, but I can't stop it.

"I want my sister back," I cry, hoping for some kind of relief. "Please, Pyotr. Please bring her back."

"I'm so sorry, Lana," he says softly. "I wish I could bring her back, but I can't." I throw myself at him, desperate to feel safe. He wraps his strong arms around me, and I bury my face into his shoulder. "I've got you. You can let it all out."

Crying. Screaming. Punching. My body rapid fires through emotions far greater than I know how to handle. Through it all, Pyotr never lets go. I cry until I'm exhausted and numb.

"It's okay to close your eyes." Pyotr strokes my forehead just like Mama does when I'm sick. "I'll keep you safe, little butterfly."

Pyotr holds me close, protecting me from the world outside. His words fill me with a sense of peace, and I know I'm safe in his arms. It's with that thought I allow myself to drift off into sleep.

When I wake, I'm in my bed. Papa's sitting in a chair next to me. He's wearing the same clothes as yesterday, and his usually perfectly groomed black hair is poking out in all directions. His eyes are still red and swollen from crying. But now there are dark circles under them. He must have sat awake all night watching over me.

"Papa," I whisper, and a fresh wave of tears spills from my eyes.

"Moya babochka." He opens his arms to me, and I crawl onto his lap. "I am so sorry I did not bring your sister back as I promised."

"It's not your fault, Papa."

"I failed—everyone." His voice trails off.

A tear rolls down his cheek, and I wipe it away with my finger. I've never seen Papa cry, and I don't like it. I wrap my arms around his neck. "Please don't cry, Papa. We're going to be okay."

We have to—for Jelena.

I don't realize I'm screaming until my door flies open, and

Pyotr's rushing into my room with his weapon drawn. "What's wrong?" he asks, panicked.

"It hurts. It hurts so badly."

He kicks the door closed and locks it before sitting beside me on the bed.

"Come here." He holds his arms out to me. And just like he did when I was a little girl, he holds me in his protective embrace as I cry for my sister. "Let it all out. I'll keep you safe, little butterfly."

Svetlana

"THANK YOU FOR SEEING ME." AFTER I COMPOSED myself from my earlier breakdown, I called Masha. Fortunately, she was able to squeeze me in as an emergency this evening.

"I'm glad you reached out." Her smile is warm. "Is it okay if Pyotr leaves?"

"No." I tighten my grip on his hand. "I want him to stay."

Pyotr has been by my side for ten years. Yes, he's paid by Papa to guard me. But he's become much more than just a guard. He's my rock and one of my best friends. The older brother I've always longed for.

"If his presence helps, he can stay." Instead of sitting behind her desk, she sits in one of the chairs by the couch. "Are you comfortable telling me what happened earlier today?"

"I remember sitting on my bed. I don't know if I fell asleep or just started remembering. But suddenly, I was eleven years old again, and it was the day I found out Jelena died." I tell her about that day and how I reacted to it today. "The few weeks following were even worse. It was like I was trapped in a nightmare, and no matter how hard I tried, I couldn't wake up. Her funeral was the hardest day of my life." I squeeze Pyotr's hand tighter. "She looked so peaceful. Like she was only sleeping. I kept watching her, hoping to see her move. Expecting that she'd sit up at any second and tell us she was fine and that there was some mistake. But that didn't happen. She didn't wake up."

For three long days, Jelena's body lays in repose. That's what Mama calls it. During this time, a steady stream of friends, family, and Papa's business associates comes to pay their final respects. The room is filled with the fragrant scent of flowers.

On the final day, Jelena's body is moved to the church for the funeral service. As the mourners enter, they file past her casket, placing flowers and kissing her forehead in a final farewell. Then, they light a candle and take their seats. The sound of people crying echoes in the big room.

Papa leads up to the front row. He sits between Mama and me, his face etched with sadness.

"Why do we have to sit up here?" I whisper to Pyotr, who's sitting beside me.

"It's the rules of a funeral."

"I don't like it." I grab his hand.

"I know, little butterfly."

The funeral service is steeped in tradition, with the priest leading us through ancient rituals and prayers. Papa argued fiercely with him about adding a more modern custom, allowing people to speak. The priest wasn't happy, but Papa won the argument.

Several people, including Jelena's teacher, have stepped forward to share their memories of my sister. Their stories all highlight Jelena's kindness, humor, and loyalty to her friends.

Right now, Innessa, Jelena's best friend, is taking her spot behind the microphone.

"I've known Jelena for almost as long as I can remember. We met on our first day of kindergarten when I was still adjusting to my new foster family. I was so scared and felt like an outsider. Jelena saw me hiding in the corner and walked right over to introduce herself. When I didn't get up, she sat next to me and started talking. Pretty soon, I was laughing and feeling at ease. Jelena

was always the brave one, and she never judged me for being a foster kid. In fact, she brought me home after school one day and asked her parents to adopt me." Papa chuckles softly beside me. "I was fortunate enough to be adopted by my foster family when I was ten years old. Jelena was there with me on that special day. She's been by my side for every major moment in my life." Innessa's voice trembles with emotion as she speaks. "Jelena is, was, my best friend. She means everything to me." She breaks down crying, and her Mama rushes over to comfort her and leads her back to their seats.

"Every now and then, I'd see Innessa somewhere. She never failed to tell me a new special memory she had of my sister."

"Knowing a loved one has not been forgotten is comforting."

"After Innessa sat down, I got up. It wasn't planned. It just happened."

"Jelena was the best sister I could've ever asked for. I have so many memories of us playing together. One of our favorite places was the tree house Papa built for us. Even though she was older than me, she always played my make-believe games and made me feel special. Jelena was also incredibly smart, and I wanted to be just like her when I grew up. I hate saying was because that means something is over. It feels like I'm admitting she's gone, and I don't want her to be gone. It's not fair that she was taken from us. I want Jelena to still be here. I don't want to do life without my sister, but I know I don't have a choice." I swipe at a tear that escapes. "It's hard to walk by your empty bedroom every day and know that you're not there. Jelena, if you can hear me, I promise to always try my best to be good and remember everything you've taught me."

I walk over to her casket, tears streaming down my face, and speak softly. Not into the microphone, but directly to my sister. "Yelena, I miss you so much. I love you, and I always will. Ya obeshchayu, ty nikogda ne budesh' zabyt"

The priest steps back up to the microphone to finish the service. He says some prayers and sprinkles some dirt and holy oil onto Jelena. The burial shroud is pulled up, covering her, and the priest reads one final scripture, Psalm 118. "Blagodarite Gospoda za to, chto On blag. Yego lyubov' dlitsya vechno."

"That was the last day I ever stepped foot in a church."

"Why do you think that is?"

"Jelena was only fifteen. She didn't do anything wrong. She was beaten and raped before some sick bastard killed her. But then, I'm supposed to believe what that priest was saying, that I should give thanks to God and that he loves us?" I shake my head. "How does that even make any sense? What kind of God lets such awful things happen? I still don't understand it, and I refuse to accept it."

"Those are fair questions. One's you're not alone in asking."

"Do you have the answers?"

"I'd be a very rich person if I did, but sadly, I don't."

After the funeral service is over, we walk behind the coffin to the graveyard. Behind us, everyone is laying Juniper branches on the road.

"Why are they doing that, Mama?"

"It's to confuse the evil spirits," she whispers.

Once we're in the cemetery, everyone gathers around where she'll be buried. I hold Mama's hand and watch Jelena's coffin being lowered into the deep hole. I can't see clearly through all my tears. When the casket is in place, everyone takes turns dropping coins and a small handful of dirt onto the casket.

"Why are they throwing money and dirt on her?" I ask Papa.

"Russians are too superstitious. But if it helps them feel better, then so be it." I decide to be like Papa and not believe in such silly things.

"That must have all been very confusing to a little girl," Masha says.

"Yes and No. It was the first funeral I'd ever attended, so I didn't know the order of events or why certain things were done. Mama, Papa, and Pyotr answered all my questions."

"I'm glad you have so many people looking out for you."

"Me too." I squeeze Pyotr's hand. "I'm a very lucky girl."

When we get back to the dorm, I decide to call my parents.

"Svetlana, I'm so glad to hear your voice," Mama answers the phone. "I'm surprised to hear from you this week, though."

"I wasn't able to leave school this time."

"Is that my little girl?" Papa calls.

"It is. I just put you on speaker, honey."

"Hi, Papa."

"How are you holding up, *moya babochka*?"

"It's been tough."

"Say the word, and I'll have the jet readied. We can be there in a few hours."

"No, I'm good. Pyotr's here. He'll make sure I'm okay."

"I was looking through our family photo albums earlier," Papa says. "I found a picture from your first day of school."

In an instant, I'm transported back in time to that day.

I finally get to go to school just like Jelena. I've been up for a long time when Mama finally comes into my room. "Svetlana, time to get up and get ready for school."

"Yes, ma'am." I hop out of bed.

"Someone's chipper today." Mama smiles.

"I'm going to school today. Just like Jelena," I squeal.

"Yes, you are. Olga's getting breakfast on the table. Run along so it doesn't get cold."

"Okay." I skip past her, and she giggles.

Jelena's already at the table waiting for me. "Good morning, Lana bug."

"Good morning." I sit next to her. "What's for breakfast?"

"It's a surprise." She grins.

I pick up my cup of hot tea and take a sip. It's nice and sweet. Olga must've put an extra lump of sugar in it this morning. The kitchen door swings open, and Olga walks out carrying two plates. She sets them down in front of us.

"Syrniki?"

"Of course." She kisses me on the head. "The first day of school is a very special occasion."

I dig into my favorite breakfast of all time. I love it so much I don't even talk during the meal.

After breakfast, Jelena and I brush our teeth in our shared bathrooms and then go to our rooms to get dressed. Mama has my new school uniform, a dark grey pinafore, and a white shirt, ironed and laid out on my bed. Next to it are white knee socks, and on the floor are my new shiny black shoes. I've been begging Mama to wear them since we bought them, but she said I had to wait for today.

I'm twirling in front of the mirror when Jelena comes into my room.

"What do you think?"

"You look like a proper schoolgirl."

One day, when I'm older, like Jelena, I'll get to wear a dark grey skirt with a button-down shirt. For now, I'm happy with the uniform I do get to wear.

"Come sit down so I can fix your hair." While Jelena braids my hair, I ask her a million questions about what school will be like.

"You'll have the same teacher I did, Ms. Zima. She's the sweetest, and you'll love her," Jelena says as she finishes one of my braids. "You'll have to find your table—"

I spin around, making Jelena drop my hair. "How will I know which table I'm supposed to sit at?"

"That's what I'm trying to tell you, silly." She turns me back around so she can rebraid that side.

"Oops."

"Ms. Zima will have name cards taped to each table so you know where to sit."

"Look at you two," Mama says as she comes into my room. "Where did my babies go?"

"I'm not a baby."

"*No, you certainly are not.*" *Mama stands next to Jelena, and I can see their reflections in my mirror.* "*You've done a beautiful job braiding your sister's hair.*"

"*Thank you, Mama.*" *Jelena beams.*

"*I have a present for you both.*" *Mama hands us each a box.* "*Go ahead and open them.*"

Jelena opens her present neatly, but I pull the lid off my box, toss it onto the floor, and find the prettiest white bows I've ever seen. I remember Jelena telling me that every year, on the very first day of school, all the girls wear the biggest white bows they can find.

"*Can you put them in?*" *I hold the bows out to Jelena as I jump up and down.*

"*May I put them in for her, Mama?*"

"*You may.*"

Jelena stands behind me and carefully clips in my bows. Then, she puts hers on.

"*I think we're going to have the prettiest bows out of everyone.*"

"*Lana bug, you can't say things like that,*" *Jelena corrects me.* "*All the girls will have equally as pretty bows. You don't want to hurt anyone's feelings.*"

"*Oh.*" *I drop my head.* "*I'm sorry.*"

"*It's okay.*"

"*We need to hurry. Papa is waiting downstairs to take your pictures.*"

"*Pictures,*" *I say and clap my hands.* "*I love pictures.*" *I take off to find Papa.*

"*Moya babochka,*" *Papa says and holds out his arms to me. When I get to him, he lifts me and spins me in the air.* "*My baby girl is going to school. What will I do all day without you?*" *He kisses my cheek and sets me on my feet.*

"*Do you need me to stay home to help you?*"

Papa laughs loudly. "*No. You must go to school. But I will be here when you get home. You can tell me all about your day.*"

"*Okay.*"

"*And look at you, malen'kiy tsvetok'.*" *Papa kisses Jelena's cheeks.*

"You look far too grown up. Maybe I should lock you in your room before the boys start calling after you."

"Oh, Papa, don't be silly."

"Can we take pictures now, Papa?" I tug on his arm.

"Outside you go," Papa says, and I grab Jelena's hand, dragging her with me.

Papa takes tons of pictures. Some of each of us alone and lots of us together. "I think I got enough." He smiles.

"Are you sure? Maybe you should take a few more."

"We have plenty of pictures. If you two don't leave now, you'll be late."

Jelena and I take turns giving Papa a hug. He wishes us luck on our first day.

"Here are your flowers, girls." Mama walks over with two big bouquets of the yummiest-smelling flowers in her arms.

"What are these for?"

"They're a gift for our teachers," Jelena says. "Everyone brings a gift for the new school year."

Mama and Papa walk us to the gates, where we quickly say goodbye to Misha and Igor, who tell us they'll watch for us when we're walking home.

"Be sure to hold your sister's hand," Mama calls as we walk away.

"I will," I yell over my shoulder.

And then we're off. We meet up with a group of girls and boys down the sidewalk a bit.

"Are you excited to start school?" Innessa asks. She's Jelena's bestest friend in the world.

"I am. Do you like my bows?"

"They're the prettiest ones I've ever seen."

"See, I told you—"

"Svetlana," Jelena says sharply. "Remember what I told you."

"Jelena says I shouldn't say stuff like that, so I don't hurt anyone's feelings."

"She's right." Innessa leans close and whispers, "So, we'll keep it our secret."

When we get to the school door, my feet stop moving.

"What's wrong?" Jelena asks.

"I'm scared. I don't think I want to go to school anymore."

Jelena makes herself smaller so I don't have to look up at her. "Being nervous is okay, but you must try it once. If it's horribly awful, I'll talk to Papa and tell him you don't ever want to come back."

"Promise?"

"Pinky promise." She holds her finger out, and I wrap mine around hers. "Come on. I'll walk you to your classroom."

"I was so scared, but Jelena walked me to my classroom and helped me find my table."

"I did not know about her promise to you," Papa says and chuckles.

"She was always looking out for me."

"From the day we brought you home from the hospital, Jelena adored you," Mama says. "She was like a little mama helping me care for you."

Talking about her, especially on the anniversary of her death, rips open old wounds. The pain is as sharp as it was the day she left us. Tears spill down my face. "I have to go. Pyotr just texted that our food arrived." I make up an excuse to hang up. "I'll talk to you soon."

"We love you very much."

"I love you both, too."

I miss my big sister. Time has not made the loss any easier to bear. I sit in the quiet darkness of my dorm room and cry. Each year, I remind myself of the promise I made to her at her funeral. *"Ya obeshchayu, ty nikogda ne budesh' zabyt.* I promise you'll never be forgotten."

Svetlana

After Jelena's passing, I was plagued with nightmares. In my dreams, she would slowly drift away from me until I couldn't recognize her face or voice. These night terrors began to seep into my waking hours. The thought of forgetting my sister terrified me.

My sister has been gone for a month. Thirty days. But it feels like an eternity. I can't imagine missing her this much for the rest of my life. Papa allowed me to take a few weeks off of school, but my tutor returned to restart my lessons last week. I guess it's a good thing. At least for a few hours, I have something to distract me from how much I miss my sister.

After my tutor leaves, Pyotr and I often go for a walk. I talk a lot about Jelena while we're out. Mama and Papa said we could talk about her whenever I wanted. But I try not to mention her because it makes them sad. Pyotr doesn't get sad, so it feels safe to talk to him. Pyotr says it'll get a little bit easier with each day that passes. I'm not sure I believe him because it hasn't gotten any better.

The other day, we took a walk to the treehouse. Pyotr said there was something he wanted to show me. When I climbed up, there was a wrapped present waiting. I tore off the paper and found a white stuffed bear. In his hands is a picture of Jelena and me.

"Squeeze his paw," Pyotr instructs.

"Hey, Lana Bug." Jelena's voice plays.

"I know how worried you've been about forgetting what Jelena sounded like. Now, anytime you want to hear her, you can."

I try my hardest not to cry, but I can't help it. "Thank you, Pyotr." I throw my arms around his neck. "This is the most special present in the whole world."

I reach over to my desk to grab the bear. Whenever I get lonely, I press his hand and hear the eternally young voice of my sister calling me Lana Bug. Holding the bear close to me, I drift back in time once again.

I don't wait for my tutor to leave before I sprint from the room and crash into something big.

"Hey, little butterfly. You're in quite a hurry."

"Sorry."

"It's okay. You didn't get hurt, did you?"

"Nope."

"Is today the big day?"

"It sure is."

"Good luck."

"Thank you." I hurry down the hall, not wanting to waste another second.

When I get to my room, I reach under my mattress and pull out my black notebook.

At the funeral, I promised Jelena I'd make sure she was never forgotten. When I made the promise, I wasn't sure what I could do to keep it. Luckily, Pyotr's pretty smart and gave me some ideas. I'd do anything to bring her back, but I can't do that. So, the next best thing is that her death might be able to help other people. I have an idea I'm hoping Papa will like.

Before I go to talk to him, I have to get changed. Papa needs to take me seriously, and he won't do that in jeans and a T-shirt. I look through my closet, but I don't have anything to wear to a business meeting.

I creep down the hall to the door of Jelena's bedroom. No one's been in here since she was taken. Slowly, I turn the handle and push the door open. It looks just like Jelena left it. Her bed is made, and all her pillows are fluffy. Her favorite stuffed animal, a brown and white stuffed horse named Sasha, is nestled in the center. She named it after Papa's American business associate Alexander, whom she had a huge crush on. On the table next to her bed is the book she was reading, *War and Peace*. It's a super big book that's required for school. I pick it up and take it with me. If Jelena was reading it, I want to read it, too.

Jelena's desk is in front of a big window overlooking the back of our property. Unlike mine, hers is neat and organized. Her math text is open, and a pencil rests in the center. Next to it is her notebook with math problems written on the page. It looks like she was in the middle of a homework assignment. It didn't matter that we were on school break. Jelena always asked for extra credit work. I don't want any more homework, but I decide I'll tidy up my desk, so it looks like hers.

The reason I came in here is to go through her closet. Jelena has clothes that are more grown-up than mine. Setting the book down, I go into her closet and search for the outfit I want—a navy blue skirt and matching jacket. Jelena wore it to volunteer at Mama's office several times. After looking through a bunch of outfits, I finally find the one I want.

My white school uniform shirt works perfectly, and even though I need to use a belt for the skirt and I have to roll up the blazer sleeves a little to make it fit, I think it works well. I pull my hair back and put it in a bun to look older. Then, after putting my black school shoes on, I grab my notebook and go downstairs to Papa's office, where I find Misha outside the doors.

"Is Papa busy?"

"He's on a phone call. Is there something I can help you with?" he asks.

"No. I need to talk to Papa about it."

"Misha, I—" Papa says, opening the door startling me. "Moya babochka, you look like you are ready to go to work."

"I am." I nod. "Do you have some time to talk?"

"For you, any time." Papa smiles and steps aside, allowing me to enter. "Please excuse me, Misha. I have an important meeting with Ms. Solonik. Can you make sure we're not interrupted?"

"Sure thing, boss."

Papa sits in his big, comfy chair with his hands folded. "What can I help you with today?"

I open my notebook and clear my throat. "I made a promise to Jelena that I wouldn't let her be forgotten."

"That will not happen."

"I know we won't forget her, but other people might. They'll forget how good she was." I pull my feet under my legs. "I don't want that to happen."

"I see. What do you have in mind?"

"I don't know for sure." I bite my lip while I look at the notes I made. "I know Jelena wasn't the only person who's ever been traf-ficked and that it happens to lots of people." I look at Papa. "Pyotr said many of the people that are taken don't have anyone who loves them or looks for them."

"That is very true."

"There has to be something we can do to help."

"You are a remarkable young lady. Do you know that moya babochka?" I shrug, not thinking I'm anything other than normal. "I have been thinking precisely the same thing."

"You have?" I ask, surprised.

"Yes. I've been busy getting some colleagues together to form a network to go after people like Rudolf Sergin and Farouk El Alami. I want to make sure no one else ever has to lose a loved one."

"I like that very much. But what about helping the people that were stolen? I want to help them."

"How so?" Papa tilts his head.

"When I was talking to Pyotr, he told me your men found other people, even kids, who'd been taken from their families."

"Yes. That is true."

"And that when they're rescued, they are usually sick or hurt." Papa nods. "Who helps them?"

"I would like to get your mama. She should be here for this conversation, don't you think?"

"Yes." I smile.

Papa texts Mama, and a few minutes later, she joins us in the office. Papa catches her up on what we've talked about so far.

"I'm on board. How can I help?" Mama asks.

"Well, you're a doctor. You can help fix whatever's hurt, right?"

"I can fix a lot, yes. But often, there are things in the mind that have been hurt. I can't fix those."

"Who can?"

"Doctors called psychiatrists and therapists."

"Can we get some of them, Papa?"

He grabs a pen and starts writing notes of his own. "Yes, I will look into hiring some mental health professionals."

"And some more doctors. I'm only one person," Mama adds. "And where are we going to do all this?"

"We are going to need a building," Papa says. "And a name."

"Yelena Nadezhda," I say.

"Jelena's Hope," Mama whispers. "I love it."

"It is perfect," Papa says. Svetlana, you have done something truly remarkable here. It is not often that adults even consider helping trafficking victims. You have created something special that will provide care and support for so many people. It shows what a tender and caring young lady you are. I am incredibly proud of you."

"As am I."

It's been a year since Jelena passed away, and today is a big day. There are so many people here to support us. It feels like the whole community is cheering us on. It's a little scary to be the center of attention.

"I wish Jelena was here."

"She is here, little butterfly," Pyotr says. "She's always watching over you."

Papa, Mama, and I are all here to cut the ribbon and officially open Yelena Nadezhda, Jelena's Hope. A special treatment center where recovered trafficking victims can come to heal. A place that will bring hope back into their lives.

My bear holds a photo, a moment frozen in time of Jelena and me. It's one of the last pictures Papa took of us over the holiday the year she was taken.

"I miss you so much," I whisper, feeling the weight of Jelena's absence in my heart. "When I first brought the idea of Jelena's Hope to Mama and Papa, I had no idea what I was really asking for. I didn't know how many families like ours were suffering or how many people were living in captivity. We've helped so many and won't stop until everyone is safe and free."

The world is darker without Jelena's bright light, but Papa is right. Jelena will never be forgotten. Her legacy lives on in each one of us.

Svetlana

After yesterday, the last thing I wanted to do was get up bright and early to go to the symposium for a session on balancing big tech versus society. I sat in the very last row so that I could get out as soon as the presentation concluded. The last thing I wanted to do was get stuck talking to anyone.

I've spent the rest of the afternoon studying for finals next week. Part of me can't wait for this term to be over. The other part is wishing it could last forever. I'm not ready to answer the questions I know are heading my way. A loud argument outside of my room interrupts my quiet study time.

"Maybe I didn't make myself clear the first time," Pyotr yells. "I will not let you in. She doesn't want to be bothered."

"I don't remember asking for permission," Slava answers equally loudly.

"This is the last time I'm going to tell you before my fist meets your face. You need to leave."

I jump from my bed and hurry to the door before there's a physical altercation. "What's going on?"

"I'm trying to tell your *boyfriend* that you don't want to be bothered."

"Svetlana, please tell your *bodyguard* to stand down?"

The men are nearly chest to chest. "It's okay." I try to slide in between them. "He can come in."

"If you need me, just call." Pyotr glares at Slava before stepping back.

"Thank you." I smile and watch him disappear inside his room.

"He lives in the dorm with you?"

"Not *with* me. He has his own room." Slava's presence inside my room makes it feel smaller than it already is. "What are you doing here?"

"I've been calling and texting all night. I got worried when you didn't answer, so I flew up to check on you."

"You didn't have to do that." Slava joins me, sitting on the bed.

"Yesterday marked the anniversary of your sister's passing. I figured this week is going to be difficult for you," he says while extending his arms. I seek refuge in his embrace, curling up against his chest. "As your Dominant, it's my responsibility to care for you, especially during difficult times."

"I miss her so much," I admit.

"I know," he replies, tracing calming circles on my back. "You don't have to carry this burden alone. Let me help ease your pain."

I allow myself to be vulnerable and release my emotions. Tears stream down my face.

Slava doesn't loosen his hold on me until I stop crying.

"Thank you," I say quietly.

"There's no need to thank me."

"Well, I'm thanking you anyway."

Slava looks around my tiny dorm room. "I don't suppose you have anything to eat in here."

"I have a few granola bars, but that's it. We're not allowed to cook in our rooms." Not that there's space for anything other than our beds and desks.

"I'd like to take you out for dinner."

"You want to take me out?"

"Why do you seem so surprised?"

"I thought we were just, you know, a contract thing."

"Svetlana," He runs his knuckles down my cheek. "I like you a lot. I'd like to have more than just a *contract thing* with you.

"Slava, you know I can't commit to anything right now."

"I know. And I'll continue to respect your boundaries. But I will also keep telling you and showing you so you have no doubt about my feelings." My stomach grumbles loudly, giving away the fact that I haven't eaten anything since this morning. "Come on, let's go."

"I can't go out like this." I motion to the sweatpants and T-shirt I'm wearing.

"You look fine."

"I wore these to bed last night."

"You win." He laughs.

While I get changed, I text Pyotr.

Me: Slava and I are going to go out and grab a bite to eat.

Pyotr: When are you leaving?

Me: I'm getting changed now. Give me five minutes.

Pyotr: Okay. I'll be out front.

Slava gives me the choice of where to eat, so I bring him to Semplice Trattoria, a small restaurant within walking distance of campus. It's mid-week, so the restaurant is empty, and we're able to get a quiet booth in the back corner.

"Finals are next week?" he asks.

"They are."

"Are you prepared?"

"I'm getting there. Between the symposium this week and everything else going on. I'm a little behind, but I'll be okay."

"I don't envy you. I'm glad my college days are way behind me."

Slava is unlike any of the men I've met in Moscow. He's much older and settled in his career. I have no doubt that if I declined my acceptance at NYU to accept his offer of a relationship, I'd be cared for and loved. I'd simply slide into his life and join him on the path he's already on. But where does that leave me, and what I want from life? If I take his offer of something more, will I end up regretting not pursuing the goals I have for my future?"

"Svetlana," Slava says, waving his hand in front of my face to get my attention.

"Can you repeat what you said?"

"I was pointing out that you haven't touched your pizza." He reaches across the table and takes my hand in his. "Would you feel better if we have this wrapped and go back to your dorm?"

"It's past visiting hours now. Maybe we can go back to your hotel?"

"We don't have to. I don't want you to feel pressured."

"I really don't want to be alone tonight."

After we get our pizza wrapped, we walk back to campus. While I pack an overnight bag, Slava gets his car.

"Are you sure about this?" Pyotr asks from my doorway.

"What do you mean?"

"You usually don't do anything this week. Are you sure you're up for this?"

I put my toothbrush in the bag and zip it closed. "Why do you seem so against me being with Slava?"

"There's a huge age difference between the two of you. I want to make sure you're not being taken advantage of."

"Really? I can't believe you would say something like that."

"I'm just looking out for your best interest."

"I don't have to answer to you about who I spent my time

with," I snap. "I'm not a child anymore. I don't need you monitoring my every step."

Pyotr holds his hands up in front of him. "I'm not trying to start a fight. I'm just—"

"I can assure you I'm not being taken advantage of." I lock the door, and we walk to the stairwell. "It doesn't really matter, though. After next week, I won't be seeing him again."

Svetlana

SLAVA'S SUITE HAS A HUGE SOAKING TUB THAT WE'RE taking advantage of. My head is laid back while I enjoy the foot massage he's giving me. I swear his fingers are magic.

"I must confess. There's another reason I flew up early. I've been waiting for the right time to tell you, but I don't think there is a right time."

"What is it?" I lift my head.

"My business in Moscow has concluded early."

"Okay?" From the tone of his voice, I can tell that isn't everything.

"My investment firm is opening a new location in Tokyo," he explains. "My partner and I take turns flying out to our new site locations. It was supposed to be his turn, but he's having a family emergency and can't go."

"What does all that mean?"

"I'm going to have to fly out."

"When?"

"My flight leaves tomorrow evening. I won't be here for our last weekend together." The past two months have flown by. We were supposed to have one more weekend together, but this news changes everything. "I can't lie. I'm disappointed that we have to end our dynamic sooner than we planned."

"I am, too." I change positions, getting on my knees and straddling his lap. "So, I guess we better make the most of tonight."

"What do you have in mind?" He grabs my ass, pulling me closer to him. His erection rubs against my pussy.

"Anything you want, Sir."

Somehow, he manages to stand us both up. I wrap my legs around him as he carries me toward the closed bathroom door. He reaches to open it, but his wet hand slides off the handle.

"Fuck it," he says, backing me up against the door. His lips crash against mine.

Slava wastes no time sliding his cock inside me. He grips my legs tightly. I'm sure there will be bruises there tomorrow. His movements are desperate—primal. It's as if he's trying to ensure I'm ruined for any other man. He comes with a deep growl, and I follow him. My inner walls squeeze his cock. He drops his forehead against mine while we catch our breath.

"That was just the appetizer," he says as he withdraws his still erect cock. "To the bed, now." He follows me. "Bend over and spread your legs."

He takes me from behind with just as much desperation as before. His hand reaches around my waist, and his fingers go to work on my clit as he works me to another orgasm. I cry out in pleasure. He pulls out and drags his finger through the wetness, spreading it to my other entrance.

The head of his cock presses against the tight muscles. I take a deep breath and relax, allowing him to enter without resistance.

"Good girl," he praises me. "You feel so fucking amazing."

I can't speak. The feel of him there is still overwhelming and takes all my concentration.

Slava grabs my hips as he begins moving. My hand slides between my legs as I pleasure myself.

"That's right, *moya nevinnyy malysh.* Make yourself come for me."

Each thrust of Slava's cock stokes the spark burning inside. As the flame grows, tension builds, and my breathing becomes erratic. A burst of white-hot sensation consumes every part of me, and everything around me fades away as shocks of pleasure pulse through my body. Slava thrusts one more time and then explodes inside me. The two of us are lost in the whirlwind of our shared orgasm.

After we've come down from our high, Slava gets in bed and pulls me against him. "I'm going to miss you, Svetlana."

My eyes close before I'm able to respond.

The bright sunlight shining through the half-open curtains wakes me. I grab my cell from the table beside the bed to check the time.

"Shit. Slava, wake up." I shake his shoulder.

"What's wrong?"

"I forgot to set my alarm. It's after nine. I'm late."

"Are you sure you have to go?" He pulls me to him, and the hair on his chest grazes my nipples. "I can come up with better ways for you to spend your time," he says between kisses.

"Yes." I kiss him. "I have to go."

"Fine." He groans but releases his hold on me. "Let's get you to school."

I shoot Pyotr a quick text.

Me: We overslept. Why didn't you call?

I get dressed while I wait for his reply.

Pyotr: You're a grown woman who doesn't need me monitoring your every step, remember?

I can't believe he's using my own words against me. I roll my eyes in frustration.

Me: I'll be ready to go in a minute.

Pyotr: I'll call for the car.

While I'm putting my hair into a messy bun, Slava's behind me getting dressed. I shift my position so I can watch the show.

"What time is your flight?"

"Six."

"Will you let me know when you've landed? I'd like to know you got there safely."

"Certainly." His lips meet mine. "I'm going to miss you."

"Me too." It's much harder to leave than I thought. But if I don't go, I'll fail the term, which can't happen. I will already have some explaining to do as to why I'm late. "I really have to go, though."

Slava walks me to the door. "I'll speak with you soon, Svetlana."

Pyotr's waiting in the hall. When he sees me, he grabs my bag and walks toward the elevator. I take a final look over my shoulder at Slava, who's standing in the doorway watching me walk away. There's something about the forlorn look on his face. It's almost enough to make me forget school and run to him. I stop walking for a brief second and look between the two men.

"You're going to be late. Are you coming?" Pyotr asks, breaking the spell.

"Yeah. I'm right behind you."

The mood in the car is tense.

"I'm sorry." I shift in my seat. "I was rude to you and shouldn't have been."

"And I'm sorry for overstepping."

My relationship with Pyotr is complex at times. He's my bodyguard, yes. But at the same time, he's so much more. We've been together for ten years. He's watched me grow up and held my hand through so many dark days. The bond we've formed is strong. It's because of that connection the lines sometimes get blurred.

"You didn't overstep. You were looking out for me. Just

because I disagree with your thoughts doesn't give me the right to lash out at you."

"I forgive you, little butterfly." Hearing my nickname gives me the confidence that everything is okay.

Pyotr drops me off outside the conference hall while he parks the car. I sneak into the already-in-progress lecture and am thankful my professor doesn't seem to notice my late entrance. I do my best to take notes and pay attention, but my mind keeps drifting back to Slava. To the look in his eyes as I was walking away.

Me: Thank you for last night. It meant a lot to me that you came.

Slava: I'd do anything for you.

My professor chooses right then to look back at me. When he sees the phone in my hand, he gives me a disapproving shake of his head. I mouth *I'm sorry* and slide my phone back into my pocket.

Svetlana

I'VE SURVIVED FINALS AND AM PACKING THE LAST OF MY things to go home.

"I can't believe we've just finished our third year," Mei says.

"I know. It's crazy, isn't it."

"When does your train leave?"

I check the clock on my phone. "In an hour."

"You should be on your way to the station. You don't want to miss your train."

"And if I do?"

"It's not too late to come home with me."

Yet again, I managed to get myself into quite a predicament. I made some major changes and didn't tell my parents about any of them. I don't know why I thought keeping them in that dark was a good idea. It didn't cross my mind at the time that, eventually, they would find out. Now, I not only have to tell them what I did, but I also have to explain why I've kept it from them. Neither of which I've quite figured out just yet.

Which is why I opted for the train. Papa wanted to send his jet to fly us home, but I was desperate for any extra time to formulate a plan. I wish Jelena were here. This is the part she always helped me with. She was an expert at talking to Papa and Mama and smoothing things over for me. No matter how many years pass, I'll never get used to living without her.

Pyotr pops his head around the door we have propped open. "Little butterfly, we need to leave now, or we'll miss our train."

Mei giggles at his childhood nickname for me.

"I'll call you when I get settled at home." I turn to Mei and give her a big squeeze. I have to fight the tears that prick my eyes. Even she doesn't know about NYU.

"Everything will be okay," she reassures me.

"I hope so." I grab my bag and head for the door. "Have a safe flight home. I'll talk to you soon."

Pyotr parks in the long-term garage, and we rush through the station to get to the correct terminal. We arrive with only minutes to spare. We're barely in our seats when the train begins to pull away.

"I'm going to take a nap. I'm pretty tired."

"Not a problem. I'll be awake."

I pop my headphones in and close my eyes, pretending to chase sleep. I didn't lie. I was out very late last night with some friends, and I'm exhausted today, but I don't have time to sleep. There are a little under four hours before I have to face my parents.

Every scenario I can imagine goes through my mind, and none of them end well. Pyotr knows I changed my major, which, in the whole scheme of things, is the lesser of the two issues I'm struggling with. What he doesn't know about is my application and acceptance to NYU. I knew Papa was going to explode, possibly literally, and I didn't want Pyotr getting in trouble. I figured if I didn't tell him, he could claim plausible deniability and hopefully escape my father's wrath. The problem with my theory is other than Masha, I've had no one to talk to about this. No one to help me come up with a solid plan.

"Are you awake?" Pyotr shakes my shoulder gently. "We're home."

I take out my headphones and pull up the shade on my window. "Already?"

"Time flies when you're snoring."

"Haha. You're so funny." I elbow him. "I can't snore if I'm not asleep."

"I'm pretty sure you were snoring. Everyone on the train was staring."

"You're lucky I like you. Otherwise, I'd have to tell Papa to fire you," I joke.

"You'd be lost without me, butterfly."

Pyotr's one of the better guards my father employs. And he's right. I wouldn't know what to do without him. I came close to not having him and almost got stuck with Viktor instead.

After Dimitri's conscription, he returned to work for Papa. When he arrived at our house, he brought Viktor. They were friends in Ukraine and served their military time together. Papa took an immediate liking to Viktor and had him shadow Pyotr, whose main job was guarding me. I didn't do much other than go to ballet lessons on Saturday. Pyotr was a highly trained guard who would've been a better asset back on his regular duty. Papa felt Viktor would be an appropriate choice for my security detail.

At the time, I was thrilled. Thirteen-year-old Lana was totally boy-crazy and only saw blond hair, blue eyes, and a gorgeous face. The fact that he was twenty years older than me and wouldn't see me as more than a child never crossed my mind. Which turned out to be a good thing. Even if I was closer to his age, I don't think I could've managed to stay in the same room with him for more than five minutes without a fight. Viktor was the most overprotective guard I'd ever met. Papa got tired of our constant bickering and decided to reassign Viktor to the United States to work with Alexander. Which meant Pyotr stayed with me.

We exit the train and wait for our bags before going outside to find the driver we're expecting. Pyotr and I are shocked to see Papa, Mama, and Misha waiting for us.

"There she is," Mama exclaims as she rushes over to me. "I've missed you so much." She squeezes me in a tight hug.

"I missed you too, Mama."

Papa takes his turn, hugging me. "You guys didn't have to meet us here."

"We couldn't wait another minute to see you." He kisses both cheeks and whispers, "It appears we have much to discuss."

I try to keep a neutral look on my face. There's no way he knows anything, right?

"Let's go to the car." Mama links her arm with mine. "I'm sure you're exhausted and eager to get home."

This is one scenario I didn't plan for.

Svetlana

MISHA SLOWS THE CAR TO A STOP IN FRONT OF OUR house. Papa gets out first and goes straight into the house. I take it as a good sign that maybe there's something important waiting for him. Misha walks in with Mama while Pyotr and I grab our bags.

"Is something going on?" Pyotr asks.

"Dunno." I feign ignorance and walk into the house.

I reach the bottom of the staircase before Papa's booming voice halts me in my tracks. "Just a minute, Svetlana." I don't turn around. "Pyotr, please take her bag. Irina and I would like to speak to our daughter in the office."

"I'd really like to freshen up after traveling first."

"It was not a request."

Pyotr takes my bag and gives me a questioning look.

"Thanks," I say and offer him a small smile before turning and walking in the direction of the office.

"Go right in. I will be there in a moment."

"Yes, sir," I mumble as I walk past him.

Mama is already seated in one of the antique armchairs across from Papa's desk. I take my seat next to her just as Papa steps into the room. I grew up playing in here and have never been afraid of my father. But right now, as he takes his place behind his oversized desk, I can't help the feeling of intimidation I'm experiencing.

"Now that we are alone." He leans forward, resting his elbows on the desk. "Perhaps you can start by explaining why you changed your course of study without telling us."

"Well," I say and fidget in my seat. "I decided to take my future career in a different direction."

"I was under the belief that you were studying business to help run Jelena's Hope." Papa keeps his voice steady and even.

"I was. Except I decided a degree in business isn't where my heart is."

"So, you transferred to the law department?" Papa asks.

"Yes. Wait. How did you know?"

"The department chair and I are colleagues. He called to congratulate me on your win in the criminal court competition contest as well as your outstanding academic success."

"Right."

"That's a lovely plan, Svetlana," Mama says, putting her hand on my arm. "Why didn't you tell us?"

"Because I didn't think you'd approve of me changing my major or the *other* part of my plan," I say quickly.

"What's the *other* part of your plan?" Mama asks.

My parents are both staring at me. I may as well be in an interrogation room with a spotlight shining on me. There's no turning back now, so I blurt it out. "I want to continue my education in New York City."

"No," Papa states firmly.

"You can't just say no. That's not fair."

"I can and did."

"Can you talk some sense into him, Mama?"

"Svetlana, you know—"

"Please, Irina. I would like to hear your thoughts on this."

After a moment of contemplation, Mama responds, "Your Papa and I were quite shocked when the department chair phoned to congratulate him on your academic success," she says, glancing briefly at Papa. "We are incredibly proud of you, of course. We wish you had told us yourself rather than us finding out secondhand. And now you're saying you're interested in attending school in the United States. It's a lot to process all at once."

"I'm not just interested. I've already been accepted. I *am* going to study there," I say firmly, bracing myself for Papa's reaction.

Papa's expression remains unreadable for a moment before he finally asks, "You did what?"

I sit up straighter, determined to stand my ground. "I applied to New York University and was accepted for the Fall term. I will be going to the United States to study."

There's a long silence as Papa processes my words. I can feel the tension in the room building, like the calm before a storm.

"Svetlana, you should go to your room so your Papa and I can talk," Mama says quietly, her eyes flickering between Papa and me.

"Gladly," I say, pushing my chair back and standing up. As I walk towards the door, I can feel Papa's eyes burning into my back. I pause for a moment and turn around. "I know you don't approve, Papa, but this is something I have to do," I say firmly and walk out of the room.

Outside, I lean against the wall and listen intently to the muffled voices coming from the office.

"You do realize how thick those doors are, right?" Misha asks.

"Shh." I strain to hear what they're saying, but it's too quiet. After a few minutes of unsuccessful eavesdropping, I give up and head back to my room, my mind already racing with plans for the future.

As I comb through my damp hair, there's a soft knock on my bedroom door.

"Who is it?" I call out.

"It's me," Mama replies. "May I come in?"

"Sure." Mama enters the room, closing the door quietly behind her. "Let me guess, you're here to scold me for arguing with Papa earlier."

She takes the comb from my hand and sits beside me on the bed. I turn towards her, allowing her to comb through my long hair. "Do you remember when I used to braid your hair at night? I miss those moments," she says wistfully. "It feels like you've grown up overnight."

"I'm still the same person, Mama."

"In some ways, yes. But you've also become so much more than the little girl who used to run barefoot through the backyard with pigtails bouncing."

I face Mama, meeting her gaze. "Have you come to tell me Papa said no to New York?"

"He hasn't made a decision yet, but that's not what I came to discuss with you."

"Okay. What is it then?"

"We saw Slava at the dungeon a few weeks ago. He mentioned that you've been spending time together in Moscow."

"Yes, we have. Is Papa upset about that, too?"

"He wasn't pleased, but Slava explained it was temporary. That's probably why he's still alive," Mama chuckles softly. "But your father and I wish you had told us about it first."

"I understand."

"I'm curious. How does Slava fit into your plans of going to the United States?"

"I don't think he does."

"Have you discussed this with him?"

"No."

"Svetlana."

"Before you say anything, please listen to what I have to say." Mama nods. "A few months ago, Slava showed up at Ecstasy. It was purely coincidental. Seeing someone familiar was comforting, and we talked all night. We spent some more time together at the club and a few weeks later decided to discuss a contract," I explain. "He's been coming to Moscow pretty much every weekend. We kinda had a dynamic going."

"Lana, there is no *kinda* in this lifestyle."

"We had a contract, but it really wasn't anything serious."

"Is that what Slava believes too?"

"I don't know." I look down and play with a loose string on my blanket. "It doesn't matter now. It's over."

"I fear you see this differently than Slava."

"What did he say?"

"It was more what he didn't say."

"What do you mean?"

"I urge you to speak with Slava. It's something for him to tell you, not me. You must be completely honest with him."

My phone buzzes with a text alert. I glance at the screen.

Slava: Have you arrived home yet?

Instead of answering, I set it face down on the bed.

Mama stands up and plants a kiss on top of my head. "The longer you wait, the more difficult it will be."

After Mama leaves, I sink back onto my pillows. I'm unsure how to have this conversation with him.

Me: I did. I meant to text but got sidetracked.

Slava: I'd like to speak to you. Can I call?

I'm not in the mood for any more *important* conversations tonight.

Me: Things are pretty tense here right now. Can we talk tomorrow?

Slava: Sure. Sleep well, *moya nevinnyy malysh.*

I drop the phone on the bed beside me and close my eyes, wishing I had someone to talk this through with. At this moment, I feel very lost and alone.

Maxim

"Irina, *vozlyublenny*, would you please pack me a bag?"

"Yes, *Gospodin*," she answers. "May I ask where you're going?"

"I am taking a trip to New York City."

A few days ago, my strong-willed daughter approached me with this seemingly crazy notion of moving to New York City. To study law, of all things. The irony of her decision is not lost on me.

At first, I was inclined to forbid her from going, but that only strengthened her resolve. I am puzzled as to why she cannot be satisfied with staying on the same continent as me. Svetlana has never been to the United States, let alone New York City, and cannot possibly comprehend the workings of a city like that. The potential danger she might be putting herself in is worrisome. How can I ensure her safety if she is halfway across the globe?

My mind inevitably drifts back to the terror-filled day ten years ago when Jelena was abducted only a few blocks from my home. It serves as a reminder that danger lurks all around. I cannot keep Svetlana locked up in her room in the name of keeping her safe. Despite my concerns, I must permit her to live her life to the fullest, even if it means allowing her to study in the United States.

After careful consideration, I arrived at an idea - Alexander Montgomery.

"You're really going to let her go?" Irina asks, surprised.

"I am."

My wife quietly continues packing clothes without arguing. "Irina." I stop her, place my hands on her shoulders, and make her look at me. "You must trust me."

"You can't guarantee her safety," she replies, her voice trembling.

"Safety is never a guarantee. You are right. But I will do everything in my power to ensure no harm comes to her."

"I trust you, *Gospodin*," she says, but her struggle is evident in her eyes.

Our daughter's abduction ten years ago changed us both. Irina quit her job as a pediatrician and fell into a deep depression while I threw myself into work. Our Dom/sub dynamic was nonexistent, and our marriage nearly fell apart. We neglected Svetlana, who had witnessed her sister's kidnapping. It took a conversation with Svetlana for me to realize the extent of her grief and the need for change.

We have done a great deal of healing. But even now, I struggle with my overprotective nature. I would prefer to keep Svetlana locked in the house where I can control every variable. But Svetlana is a tenacious young woman who challenges me constantly. I will never tell her, but my daughter keeps me in check. I can't stifle her dreams, even if it means letting her go to New York City.

It has been almost a decade since the night I walked into Alexander's office only to find a young, inexperienced, and broken young man sitting behind a desk. His business was failing, and he was ready to throw in the towel and call it quits. I offered him an opportunity to join forces with me in my fight against human trafficking. I do not know if he was brave or just desperate, but he agreed.

Me: I just landed at JFK. Do you have time to meet with me today?

Alex: I'll clear my schedule. Where do you want to meet?

Me: Fire and Ice. I can be there in an hour.

Alex: See you then.

Over the years, we have worked closely, and he has taken on more responsibilities in my business. I have had the privilege of watching Alexander heal and grow in confidence. He has more than proven himself to be a trustworthy man. And, for the most part, gets along well with Svetlana. A necessary skill to possess for what I am about to ask.

Alex

MAXIM'S TEXT REQUESTING I MEET HIM AT FIRE AND Ice has disrupted my plans for the afternoon.

"Can you clear my schedule this afternoon?" I ask my office assistant Paul.

"Sure, Mr. Montgomery."

"Thanks."

"Is everything okay?"

"I hope so." I have a secure line in my home office. That's the usual method of communication for something important. The fact that Maxim's flown in from Russia without warning has me concerned. "Hey, Brand." I pop my head into his office. "I'm going to be heading out in a few. Paul's rescheduling this afternoon's meetings." Over the past few years, Brandon has become not only my best friend but also an irreplaceable part of my company.

"What's going on?"

"Maxim just texted. He's in the city and asked me to meet with him."

"I didn't know he was in town."

"Me either. I'll be at Fire and Ice if you need me."

"Let me know how it goes."

Viktor pulls up in front of the club, and as I step out of the car, I spot Timur leaning against the building. He appears to be engrossed in his phone, trying to blend in with the crowd. However, I know better than to think he's just another New Yorker buried in their device. His eyes are constantly scanning the area for any threats of danger.

"Nice to see you, Alex."

"You too."

"The boss is inside."

"Has he been waiting long?"

Timur checks the time on his phone. "Only about fifteen minutes."

"Viktor's parking the car. He'll be here in a few minutes."

Since the club is closed, it's easy to spot Max sitting in the café. He stands when he sees me.

"Thank you for meeting with me on such short notice."

"It's not a problem." I take my seat. "Is everything okay?"

A server arrives with our meals.

"I took the liberty of ordering for us." Once the server leaves, Max reveals the reason for his impromptu visit. "Svetlana has been accepted at New York University."

"Congratulations."

"I wish I could share in your excitement." Maxim's lack of enthusiasm doesn't surprise me. I've known Svetlana since she was a girl. She's always been an intelligent and independent young woman. Which is part of the problem. Svetlana has a mind that is very much her own. She never backs down from an opportunity to challenge her father. Max will never admit that she gets her strong-willed nature from him. Even though he's struggling with her choice, he adores her, and I'm sure he's proud of her achievements. "It has been a lot to process."

"That's understandable. But I'm sure she'll do great there."

"Yes. I have no doubt."

Max eats in silence for a few minutes. I know he didn't fly all the way to New York to tell me Lana would be attending college here. He doesn't seem in a hurry to tell me what is going on, though. I've known Max for long enough to realize I need to be patient, but curiosity is about to get the better of me.

"As you know, Svetlana is in the lifestyle."

"Yes," I answer hesitantly, unsure where he's going with this.

"She is a submissive without a Dominant."

"Maxim, I'm not interested in having a—"

"I am only asking if you will be her protector. And her friend," he says. "I'm planning to send Pyotr with her, but I need to know she will have someone familiar with the city and the people at Fire and Ice."

I don't know what I expected Max to say, but it wasn't this. "What would agreeing to this entail?"

"I trust you to oversee any Dominants who express interest in approaching Svetlana. As someone familiar with both the individuals here and Svetlana herself, I am confident that you will prioritize her safety and well-being in this matter."

"She would wear my collar of protection?"

"If you agree, yes."

I run my hand through my hair. A collar of protection is much different than a permanent collar, but I'll still be responsible for another person. This is not a simple yes or no question. "Can I take some time to think about it?"

"Of course. If you did not ask for time, I would be worried."

"When is she planning to arrive?"

"We have not discussed that yet. Alexander, I understand the gravity of what I am asking."

"I know you do. I'll have an answer for you tomorrow."

We spend the remainder of our meal discussing business. One of the most recent events is that Irina left her position in the pediatric office where she's worked for years. She's not the medical director for Jelena's Hope.

"Leaving her private practice must have been difficult for her."

"It was. As much as she loved working with the children, her heart is at Jelena's Hope. She was exhausting herself going back and forth."

"She's a hard worker. This will ease things up for her." I take a drink of water. "How long are you in town for?"

"Only a few days."

"I'll have my housekeeper get a guest room ready."

"Timur reserved a suite at the Ritz-Carlton."

"There's no need for that. You're always welcome at my home."

"I do not want to be an imposition."

"I have plenty of room, and Timur can stay downstairs with Viktor."

"Thank you, Alexander. I appreciate your hospitality."

Brandon

ONCE AGAIN, I FIND MYSELF WORKING LATE IN THE office, but I don't mind. There are still moments when I wonder how fortunate I was to land a job like this. Memories of my first encounter with Maxim Solonik and Alex come to mind.

By the time I get to Fire and Ice, the lobby is empty except for Star and two large men who appear to be guarding the main doors of the club.

"Good evening, Star. What's with the security?" I motion with my chin.

"We have a guest tonight."

"Must be someone important."

"Maxim Solonik. He's been here a few times."

"I've heard his name mentioned in passing." This is the first time I'm here the same night as this mysterious Russian.

"He has a great reputation at his dungeon in Russia. Maxim is also a whip master," Star says, getting my attention. "He's teaching a special class."

"Sounds like I came on the right night.

"He also brought a young man with him—Alexander. He lives in the city but has been struggling after the death of his mother.

Maxim seems to have taken him under his wing. Maybe you can introduce yourself?" she asks, uncertain.

"I'll be sure to find him."

"Excellent. So, are you here to play or just a voyeur tonight?"

"Just here for dinner and show." We share a laugh.

"In that case, enjoy your evening." She nods at the guards, who step out of my way so I can enter the club.

Working in Brooklyn and having to drive across town to get here takes forever. So, by the time I step into the main room, tonight's action is already underway. My first stop is the café. I'm starving. Lucky for me, it seems most everyone is gathered around the stages tonight, so I get a table right away. While I eat, I watch the scenes.

Vivian, one of the club's regular Domme's, is doing a teacher/student scene with her sub, Haven. It seems the student hasn't been achieving her full potential in class and has landed in detention. The teacher is educating her with a violet wand. Given the pleasure-filled moans coming from the stage, it's clear the ladies are both having a good time.

Stage two's scene is just getting started. Master Emiliano is prepping his slave, Avalon, for her punishment. The two had been in a Dom/sub dynamic for several years but recently have transitioned into a Master/slave dynamic. Although Avalon was the driving force to take their relationship to the next level, she's struggled to get used to her new role. Emiliano is patient, but only so much can be tolerated—even in a learning situation. There are rules and boundaries in place for a reason. Their dynamic will fail if Emiliano doesn't follow through with the punishments spelled out in their contract.

On stage three, I spot Maxim Solonik. He's taking some practice swings with his whip, no doubt warming up his arm. I'm glad I haven't missed his class.

As I finish my meal, I attentively listen to the experienced Dominant as he discusses the different grips and stances a person can take while using a whip. Then, he demonstrates using the various instruments.

"He's very impressive," I say quietly as I take the last empty seat by the stage.

"Maxim has a lot of experience."

"You know him?"

"I do." The guy sticks his hand out. "Alex Montgomery."

"Brandon Carpenter. Nice to meet you."

I return my attention to the stage. The whip is my impact implement of choice. I've taken several classes and have become comfortable using it. My goal is to become as skilled as the man on the stage. It's clear he has a wealth of knowledge that he's eager to share with anyone willing to learn.

"That concludes my demonstration." He pauses while his audience applauds. "Would anyone be interested in doing some one-on-one work?"

My hand shoots up. There's no way I'll pass up an opportunity like this. It appears I'm the only one who's volunteered and am invited onto the stage. After a quick introduction, Maxim has me choose the whip I'm most comfortable with.

"I am interested in why you chose this particular tool."

"The stock whip is the one I learned first. I'm comfortable with the level of control I have when using it. And—" I hesitate. "I get a certain amount of satisfaction watching a restrained submissive squirm when she hears the crack. They're often unsure of how much it'll bite and are surprised when the sting isn't as big as the sound."

"That is a good assessment. I would like to see your technique."

He steps a safe distance away. I'm confident in my movements and precision with the stock whip. With every swing, I skillfully adjust the intensity of impact and strike my intended target with accuracy. "Very good," Maxim says. "I would like to see you wield a bullwhip."

"I've never used one."

"There's a first time for everything. Would you like to learn?" Maxim asks me.

I'm at a crossroads, faced with a choice I knew would come at some point. Do I continue to avoid it out of fear, or do I take the leap and reclaim this part of me? "Yes, I'd love to."

Maxim brings two chairs from the audience to the stage and suggests we sit down and go over the basics of the bullwhip. He starts by explaining the history of its design and then demonstrates the best ways to execute a strike. After finishing, he hands me the whip and says, "Let's see what you can do."

Nervously, I take a few swings, but Maxim interrupts, "Wait. Try holding it like this." He adjusts my grip on the handle, explaining that it will give me better control and produce a louder crack.

Following his advice, I'm able to precisely hit my target and create a louder sound each time. I continue to practice until my arm tires, and my accuracy begins to falter. "I think I need to stop for a while. My arm is done."

"That was a good call. Many Dominants are so focused on their submissive that they fail to see the signs their body gives to end a scene."

I look out into the club and realize it's empty. The only people left are Star and Montgomery, who are sitting in the chairs watching. "I'm sorry, Star. Time seems to have gotten away from us."

"Not at all. Alex and I were enjoying chatting."

"You are always most hospitable, Mistress," Maxim says with a smile.

Not wanting to keep Star any longer, we quickly clean up the stage. I hate that it's gotten late and the instruction has ended. There's so much more I can learn from Maxim.

"Would you care to grab a bite to eat?" I ask as we exit the stage.

"Thank you for the invitation, but I am no longer a young man. I am going to head back to my hotel and get some much-needed sleep. Alexander, maybe you would like to join Brandon in my place?"

"Do you mind?" he asks.

"Not at all." I turn to Maxim. "Thank you again."

"It was my pleasure."

We wait with Star while she locks up.

"May I offer you a ride home?" Max asks Star.

"That would be lovely."

Alex and I see them off and then head out for something to eat and a few drinks. We sit in the quiet back corner of a little bar situated in a fancy upper-West side neighborhood. Although I don't live here, this is my bar of choice when I want to escape the constant noise and craziness of Manhattan.

"How do you know Maxim?"

"He's a business associate." Alex takes a swig of his beer.

This strait-laced guy and the Russian are business associates. Something doesn't add up. "What do you do?"

"I own a marketing firm—Montgomery Advertising." He quickly changes the subject. "Have you always lived in the city?"

"I was born and raised in Brooklyn," I respond to Alex's question. He watches me closely, waiting for me to elaborate. My story's not all that interesting, but here goes. "I have a sister, Quinn, who's eighteen years older than me. Needless to say, I was a bit of a surprise for my parents, who thought their days of raising children were over. Instead, they found themselves parents of a newborn. Quinn had already moved out of the house by the time I was born. She and I aren't very close." I stop and take a drink. "My parents were wonderful people and hard workers. Two years ago, Mom had a major heart attack and passed away. Dad never recovered from the loss and died six months later."

"I'm sorry to hear that. That must've been rough."

"I guess that's one of the worst parts of having older parents. Having to say goodbye too soon." I shrug.

"Does your sister still live in the city?"

"No. Her husband is career military. Currently, he's stationed in Germany, so they and their three kids are there. We talk every now and then, but that's about it."

"So, you're pretty much on your own here."

"I am."

"*What do you do for work?*" he asks.

"*I graduated high school and slipped right into the role of care-giver for my parents. The city's a pretty expensive place to live, so I'm currently working a few odd jobs.*"

Alex leans forward, resting his elbows on the table. "*What would you think about making a career switch?*"

"*Considering I don't have an actual career, I'm open to hearing the details.*"

"*Come work for me at my firm.*"

"*I don't know anything about marketing.*"

"*I can teach you what you need to know.*"

"*You don't even know me. Why would you offer me a job?*" Either this guy's drunk, or he's just plain crazy.

"*I have a feeling about you.*"

I raise my eyebrow and consider that my second thought must be right—he's crazy.

"*It wasn't long ago someone took a chance on me. If that hadn't happened, I would've been forced to close up shop and move back to Seattle.*" He sits back. "*So, what do you say? Will you come work for Montgomery Advertising?*"

"*What the hell, sure.*"

Brandon

My cell rings as I walk into my house.

"He wants me to agree to be a protector Dom for his daughter, Svetlana," Alex says.

"Hello to you, too."

"Hi."

"A protector Dom. Wow. That's a big ask."

"It is. But she'll be busy at school most of the time."

"You're actually considering this?"

"I am."

"You're crazier than I thought."

"That just might be true," he laughs.

"Are you going into the office tomorrow?"

"No. Max is staying at my place."

"Okay. I'll catch up with you on Monday then."

Nothing Maxim Solonik does is anything less than over the top. Even though I should be used to his way of doing things, I can't help but be shocked.

First thing Monday morning, I find myself in a dress shirt and tie as I walk into Montgomery's office to report for my first day of work.

I step off the elevator and into Montgomery Advertising. A younger guy sits behind the desk. He's currently on a call, so I stand off to the side and wait.

The office takes up the entire floor. Down the right side of the space are doors that I'm assuming lead to private offices. The center is open with lots of natural light from the building's windows. Desks are arranged in groups of four. Several people sit at their computers, appearing to be hard at work. I gotta say, I'm impressed with the place.

"Brandon?" the guy asks when he hangs up.

"Yes."

"Sorry for keeping you waiting. I'm Paul. It's nice to meet you." He extends his hand. "Mr. Montgomery is expecting you. His office is the last door on the right."

"Thanks."

"Thank you," I reply, aware of the curious stares from employees as I walk past them. Despite feeling out of my depth, I resist the urge to turn back and go home.

"Good morning," Alex greets me as he opens his office door.

"Morning," I reply.

"Please come in," he says, gesturing me inside.

To my surprise, Maxim is sitting on a black leather sofa. He stands up to greet me. "It's good to see you again, Brandon."

"Likewise," I reply and take a seat in a sleek leather chair. Alex sits down at his desk and gets straight to the point.

Montgomery didn't specify the position when he asked me to work for him. I came in anticipating discussing something entry-level where I'd be filing, photocopying, and making coffee, but that's not what is being described.

"I'd like to offer you the position of Chief Marketing Officer," he says.

"Wait a minute," I interrupt. "I think you misunderstood what I told you last night. I don't have a college degree or any experience in marketing."

"I didn't misunderstand." Alex leans back in his chair.

"I guess it's me that doesn't understand."

"Alexander does a great deal of work for me." Maxim joins the conversation. "Due to the sensitive nature of my accounts, my business cannot be handled by just anyone. As Alexander already knows, I have high requirements for an employee."

"Neither of you knows me. Why would you offer me a job like this?"

"We don't know you personally. You are correct. But my sources have informed me that you fit the description."

His sources? Who is this guy? "I get the feeling there's more to this job offer than meets the eye."

Maxim tells me about his daughter, Jelena. Then, he provides a detailed explanation of his business operations. As it turns out, Maxim's a powerful player in the Russian Bratva. He leverages Montgomery's company to distribute sensitive information to a network of individuals working together to combat the global issue of human trafficking.

"Why me?"

"I got a feeling about you, and I've learned to trust my gut on these things," Alex says matter-of-factly. "If you need some time to think about it—"

"I'm in." Rarely do I go with my gut reaction. I'm more of a think things through until I have a contingency plan for my contingency plans. For some reason, this is different. There's a voice urging me to say yes. That this is something I need to be involved in.

"You did not ask about salary," Maxim adds. Rising from his seat, he grabs a pen from the desk and writes something on a piece of paper before sliding it over to me. I'm shocked when I pick it up. Confident that he put too many zeros on the number, I go to open my mouth, but Max stops me.

"There is no amount of money too great in this fight."

. . .

Alex and Maxim spend the next few hours explaining how the network operates and outlining my role within it.

"We'll be working closely together, and in six months, you'll be a marketing expert," Alex says.

"I'll take your word on that."

"Come on, I'll show you to your new office." Which is just a few doors down from his.

The nameplate on the door reads 'Brandon Carpenter.' The office is almost as large as Montgomery's, with a stunning city view. A large modern desk with an ergonomic chair sits in front of the windows. The wall to the right of the desk is lined with bookshelves.

"Through this door is our shared conference room, and that door"—He points to a second door— "leads to your private bathroom."

"Right." My head is spinning.

"I know how overwhelming this all is. I felt the same way when all this was getting off the ground."

"Overwhelming is putting it mildly."

"Max has a big personality. He can be a lot," Montgomery chuckles. "But he's a really good guy who's doing some very important work."

"I guess I'm still trying to figure out why me." I lean against the desk.

"When he first approached me, I had the same questions. I've since learned that fate has a way of bringing the right individuals together at the right moment," he responds before walking back to the door. "There's a paper on your desk with the company login information and a website. Order whatever you want to furnish your office. After you're settled here, head up to Human Resources. They're on the next floor up. They have all your onboarding paperwork. You're free to go when you're done there."

"Thank you. I really appreciate this opportunity."

"You're welcome." Alex raps his knuckles on the door frame. "I'll see you tomorrow."

I sit behind my desk and attempt to let the reality of all this set in. If you had told me when I walked into Fire and Ice on Friday that I would be offered a new job, and not just any job, one that could change my entire life, I would've said you were crazy. But here I am.

As I leave my office, I feel a newfound sense of purpose. I've been given the opportunity to work on a project that's bigger than me. Fate put us together, and I get the feeling she isn't done with me yet.

Alex

TIMUR MAY BE OLDER THAN VIKTOR AND ME, BUT THAT didn't stop him from kicking our asses in my private gym. I'll never question Maxim's choice of guards again. On the way to my room for a shower, I pass my office, where I hear Max on the phone. Judging by the tone of his voice, I'd hate to be whoever's on the receiving end. Max was planning to stay in town for a few days, but he received an urgent call late last night that has him rushing to prepare his jet for an immediate return home.

While I shower, I contemplate Max's request to take Svetlana on as a protected submissive, a decision that kept me up all night. My first instinct was to say no. The idea of being responsible for someone else's well-being is daunting. However, Max has been a steadfast friend and mentor to me. The night Maxim walked into my tiny office changed my career. I was days away from going bankrupt and having to return to Seattle as a failure. I owe the success of my company to him.

As if that wasn't enough, eight years ago, Max found me at my lowest. It was the first anniversary of my mom's passing, and I was a drunken mess. Maxim understood such profound grief and didn't judge my poor coping mechanism. Instead, he sat with me all night while I sobered up. Then, he brought me to Fire and Ice and re-introduced me to the lifestyle I'd turned my back on.

Although I've remained a member and visit the club a few times a month, it's usually to observe. I've done a few non-sexual scenes, but that's as far as it's ever gone. Having a permanent submissive is a big commitment. Too often, feelings get in the way, and when that happens, it leaves open the possibility of getting hurt. That's not an avenue I'm interested in pursuing.

So, why am I still considering it? It's not because I'm interested in Lana, even though I get the feeling Max wouldn't be opposed to that. I know he'd never hold it against me if I declined his request. But there's something else, something bigger than gratitude toward him, that's urging me to say yes.

Svetlana will have two more years of school left when she transfers to NYU. Then, I'm assuming, she'll return to Russia. So, this isn't long-term. But am I able to make a commitment to being a protector Dominant? By the time I finish dressing, I'm confident with my answer.

When I emerge from my room, I find my office door open. The three men are in my kitchen, discussing something in hushed tones.

"Alexander," Max says when he sees me. "Thank you for letting me use your office."

"I hope everything's okay."

"There are some developments at the center that need my personal attention."

I lean against the counter opposite the island where Maxim sits with a cup of coffee. "Do you have a few minutes to talk before you leave?"

"We're going to get the bags in the car. Let us know when you're ready to go," Viktor says as he and Timur leave the room.

"I've given your request a great deal of thought. If Svetlana is agreeable, I will be her protective Dominant."

"Thank you, Alexander. This eases my mind a great deal."

Max's body visibly relaxes. "I will speak with my daughter when I arrive back home."

Svetlana

"Svetlana," Papa says when I come up for air.

"I didn't know you were home." I push myself onto the side of the pool.

"I got in a short time ago." He passes me a towel. "I would like to speak with you."

"About?"

"Dry yourself and get dressed. We will talk in my office."

"Okay. I'll be there in a few minutes."

I guess I'm done swimming laps today. Papa said he was going to New York for business, but I'm hopeful at least part of the trip was to consider my request to study there.

After I've dried and dressed, I pad barefoot through the house and find Timur outside the office.

"The boss is waiting for you." Timur opens the door for me.

"Thanks, T." I smile nervously and walk into Papa's office.

"Take a seat, *moya babochka*."

I sit, tucking one leg under me. My fingers trace the ornate carvings on the antique chair. "Did you have a good trip?"

"I could have used more time with Alexander, but there was some business I had to return to deal with."

"What's going on?"

Since the day I asked Papa about Gavriil's involvement in Jelena's abduction, he's allowed me to know bits and pieces about his business. Of course, I wanted to learn more. Over the years, I've pushed, hoping to take on a more significant role. That's part of the reason I chose to study business. I thought if I did that, Papa would finally give in and allow me to be a part of his organization. But he refuses. He's adamant that women do not hold positions in the Bratva. I'm all for breaking stereotypes, but Papa is not.

"Nikolai Federov's men busted a trafficking ring and apprehended someone we have been after for a long time."

"He couldn't handle it on his own?"

"Federov knew I would want to deal with this personally."

"It was someone involved with Jelena's kidnapping, wasn't it?" Even though she's been gone for a decade, Papa has not given up on tracking down every last person involved.

"Yes. She was the one person who has evaded us all these years."

"She? It was a woman?" That news rattles me. How could another woman participate in an act so disgusting?

"This is not what I brought you in here to discuss." Ugh. Papa's a master at shutting down and changing the subject. "I have made a decision on you going to New York?"

"I already told you. I'm going whether you ag—"

"Svetlana." Papa holds his hand up, silencing me. "I went to make arrangements with Alexander for your arrival."

"You did?"

"You may go on certain conditions."

Here we go. "What are they?"

"You will stay with Alexander until the dorms open at the end of August, and Pyotr will accompany you. I'll make arrangements for him to live on campus."

"I don't want a guard with me."

"We are not having this argument, Svetlana."

"Papa, I need the opportunity to live on my own. I'm asking you to trust me."

"My dear daughter." Papa softens his voice. "It is not you that I distrust. It is others that seek to do harm that I do not trust."

"I know all too well the evil that exists in the world. It was me that was with Jelena when she was taken. I watched her be dragged away." I swallow the knot that's forming in my throat. "When I open my eyes each morning, I renew my vow to live despite whatever danger may be around the corner. If I didn't, fear would rule my life, and evil would win. I can't let that happen."

I'm just about to give up hope when Papa speaks. "There is not a day that goes by that I do not thank God you were spared. I know how close I came to losing both of my girls that day. And yes, at times, it has made me a little overprotective."

"A little?"

"Well, maybe a little more than a little bit." Papa smiles. "But you have made an excellent point. I am willing to offer a compromise."

This is progress. "What are you proposing?"

"For my sake, Pyotr will accompany you at all times, but he does not have to live in your dorm."

"No. Going to New York is meant to be a fresh start. I can't do that with security following me around."

"I am willing to have him out of sight. As long as he's there."

"Totally out of sight?"

"Totally out of sight."

A smile spreads across my face. "It's a deal."

"On to the next point. Alexander."

Papa informs me that Alex has agreed to be my protector Dominant. I feel a tinge of embarrassment, knowing that he went behind my back to arrange it. Rather than resist, I decide to accept his offer. It's my part of the compromise for Papa not forcing Pyotr to live in the dorm with me. I'll deal with Alex once I get there.

"Thank you for doing that, Papa. I appreciate you looking out for me," I say, grateful for his concern. "When can I leave? I'd really like to explore the city before school starts."

"Alexander is willing to accommodate your schedule."

I pull out my phone and open the calendar app. I want to pack and leave tomorrow, but I suspect Papa will have something to say about that. "How about the first week of July?"

"That works well. I will inform Alexander of your plans."

"This means a lot to me. Thank you, Papa."

Brandon

"I CAN'T BELIEVE YOU AGREED TO THIS. YOU'RE CRAZY."

Alex shrugs. "Possibly. But if I was in his shoes, which I never will be, I'd hope someone would do the same thing for me."

Alex has known Svetlana since she was a young girl. I've never met her, but he's told me countless stories about what a handful she is. You'd think she would've outgrown it, but it doesn't seem like she has. She sounds like a spoiled little rich girl to me. There's no way I would've agreed to babysit her.

"When is she coming?"

"She'll be here the first week of July."

"So, these are your last few weeks of being single." I chuckle.

Alex rolls his eyes. "Lana and I aren't a couple. I'm just going to be looking out for her."

"We'll see about that."

"I'm sure you have work or something to do. " I don't want to keep you," Alex says, heading to my office door. "I have an errand to run."

"Are you going anywhere fun?"

"The jeweler to pick up her collar."

"You're going to collar her?" I'm beginning to think he's completely lost his mind.

"A protective collar, yes. If I'm doing this, I'm doing it right."

I've been too busy ribbing Alex to notice the tension in his body. He's taking this very seriously, and it's already weighing heavily on him. I close my laptop. "Actually, I don't have anything pressing to do. How about I go with you?"

"Thanks. I'd appreciate the company."

He's quiet as we ride down the elevator and exit the building. Once we're outside, he lets out a big sigh.

"You good?"

"I don't know. This is a big commitment. I don't want to do anything to screw it up. If something happens to her on my watch."

"You aren't going to let anything happen to her."

"I'll do my best, but I'm only one person."

"I've got your back."

"Really?"

"Of course."

"Thanks." He slaps my shoulder.

Rather than take the subway, Alex and I walk the ten blocks to the small jewelry shop.

We aren't all the way into the store when a curvy brunette spots Alex and bats her fake eyelashes at him. "Mr. Montgomery. It's so nice to see you again."

"Harvey called to let me know my order came in." Alex ignores the woman.

"Yes, it did. I'll go get it." She turns and sways her hips as she walks into the backroom.

"Someone's happy to see you," I whisper.

"She's married."

"That doesn't seem to matter to her."

"I know."

"Here it is," she says as she approaches us.

Alex takes the offered velvet box and lifts the lid. "What do you think?" Inside the box is a delicate chain. A silver charm with a garnet dangles from it. A lowercase p and the initials A.M. are engraved on it. "I wanted it to be something she can wear to school without attracting unwanted attention," he explains.

"Because a garnet is discreet?"

"It's her birthstone."

"That makes more sense."

"Do you like it?"

"I'm flattered, but I don't think it's my color," I grin, and Alex rolls his eyes.

"Do you think she'll like it?"

"Yes. I think Lana will love it."

Whether or not Lana likes this collar is of little interest to me. I'm more concerned about whether Alex has gotten himself in over his head. He hasn't had a submissive since I've known him. Not only hasn't had one but also hasn't been the least bit interested in finding one. Now, this. I'll give him that it's for protection, but women get attached easily. Svetlana will want more from him, and knowing Alex, he'll cave and try to give it to her. This can only end one way—disaster.

Svetlana

DELAYING MY DEPARTURE UNTIL JULY TURNED OUT TO be a wise choice as it allowed me to get everything ready without rushing to leave for New York City. Over the past few weeks, I've purchased most of the things I need for my dorm. For convenience's sake, I'm having them shipped directly there.

Now that the move is approaching, my excitement has turned to nerves. I enjoyed living in Moscow, but it wasn't a true test of my independence. Moving to New York City is both exciting and terrifying.

I am also faced with the dilemma of Slava, an issue I've yet to tackle. We've had some contact since our contract expired. He's still in Japan and has asked me several times to fly out and visit him. Slava has mentioned he'd like to discuss another contract. Although I enjoyed my time with him, accepting his offer would mean giving up everything I've worked so hard for. That's not something I'm willing to do. I have to figure out something, though. He doesn't know I'm leaving in two days, and I'm unsure how to tell him.

"Svetlana," Mama says, popping her head into my bedroom. "Are you ready to go?"

"I just have to grab my shoes."

Any decisions about Slava are going to have to wait. Today, Mama and I are doing some last-minute shopping for new clothes and shoes. Although I was content with waiting until I got to the city, Mama insisted on the one-on-one time, which I don't want to miss. Once I leave, it'll be a while until I see her. She can't just up and leave Jelena's Hope without having enough staffing to care for the people we have there. I can't think about stuff like that, or I may lose my nerve.

Even though I know Pyotr and Misha hate shopping, they've been extra patient today and even pretended to enjoy themselves. I'm sure Pyotr hopes this means I won't drag him shopping when we get to New York. I don't want to burst his bubble yet. He'll find out soon enough that I plan on taking full advantage of shopping in a new place.

Our last stop is for a late lunch at a lovely little café. The guys grab a table in the corner, giving Mama and me privacy.

"I can't believe you're leaving in two days. The month seemed to go by so quickly."

"Neither can I. But I'm really excited to go."

Mama watches me intently. "You don't look like someone who's excited."

Before I can respond, the server appears with our food. I wait until she's gone before I speak. "New York University is a highly regarded institution. This is the opportunity of a lifetime, and I know how lucky I am. But at the same time, I'm leaving my family and everything I know behind."

"Did you have these doubts when you applied to the school?"

"No. I suppose I didn't think it through very well."

"Or is it perhaps that your circumstances have changed since then?"

"What do you mean?"

"Does Slava have anything to do with your current reluctance to go?

"Our contract ended, and then he left for Japan."

"But you keep in touch."

"We do."

"What does he think about you leaving?"

I knew this was going to come up. I promised Mama when I came home from Moscow that I'd have this conversation with Slava, but I never did. "He doesn't know."

"Svetlana." Mama's voice is stern. "I thought we discussed this."

"We did. But since our dynamic is over, I didn't see the need to tell him."

"It may be over on paper, but you know as well as I do that there are still unresolved feelings between you. You owe it to Slava to be completely transparent. Honestly is one of the keys to how this lifestyle works."

"I wasn't dishonest with him."

"Withholding information is dishonesty," Mama says sharply. "I know you say you want to be a submissive, but if you aren't prepared to be honest at all times, then perhaps you should consider if this lifestyle is really where you belong."

I can't believe she'd even suggest that. "Our contract was a short-term arrangement. Nothing serious. There was no need to tell him about New York."

"I disagree. There's more to it than *nothing serious*." I shrug. "I saw the look on his face when he spoke about you. That man is very taken with you. Whether he's said the words or not, he's hoping for something more serious."

"I guess."

"He's a good man."

"I know, and I'd have a solid future with him." I sigh. "The problem is, if I agree to a long-term dynamic with him, I'd be giving up the things I want."

"You wouldn't go to New York to study, but there are schools in Japan. Slava won't hold you back. As your Dominant, he'll want to see you flourish."

I pick at the food on my plate while I think about what she's said. How Slava would react isn't something I've given much consideration to. The only thing I thought about was not going to New York. "I guess not."

"Have you spoken to Czarenah about this?"

"No."

"Why not?"

"We haven't spoken in months. She didn't tell you?"

"No, she didn't." Mama looks surprised.

I add to her disappointment by explaining how I cut Czarenah out of my life because she disagreed with me.

"I'm beginning to think Czarenah may have been right," Mama says.

"And that's why I didn't tell you. I knew you'd take her side."

"It's not about taking sides. We all care about you and don't want to see you get hurt."

"Can we change the subject? I don't want to spend my last few days at home arguing with you."

Mama steers the conversation toward the upcoming developments at Jelena's Hope. The center is expanding by adding elementary school classrooms to accommodate the increasing number of young children needing rehabilitation. The children we recover require a supportive and specialized learning environment. Their unique needs cannot be met in a traditional school setting.

While it's a significant undertaking, my parents are glad to support it. However, it's also a bittersweet moment. More children being recovered means more are being sold into slavery, and their young lives are forever changed. Jelena's Hope having to grow isn't something that excites any of us. We're just grateful that our center can provide the necessary support and care to meet their needs.

<h1 style="text-align:center">Svetlana</h1>

Misha pulls up to the tall wrought iron gates that grant entrance to our property. They slowly open, allowing our vehicle to pass through. As we get closer to the front of our house, I notice an unfamiliar car parked in front.

"Are we expecting company?"

"Not that I'm aware of," Mama answers.

It takes the four of us to carry all my packages. I'm going to need another suitcase for all this stuff. We're barely ten steps into the foyer when Timur appears.

"Lana, your father would like to see you. He's in the library."

"I'll get these." Pyotr takes my bags. "Do you want them in your room?"

"Yes, please." I look to Mama. "Are you coming?"

"No. Your papa only asked for you." That wasn't the answer I was hoping for. And why is he in the library? Normally, he uses his office for business. "Do you know what he wants?" I ask Timur as we walk down the hall.

"I'm not at liberty to discuss it."

"Go figure." I blow out a frustrated breath. But as soon as I step into the entrance to the library, all my questions are answered. "Slava, what are you doing here?"

He stands and walks over to greet me with a kiss on my cheek. "I wanted to speak with you. In person."

Papa rises from his chair. "It was good catching up with you, Slava. I will leave you two to talk."

"Thank you, Max."

Papa closes the door behind him, leaving Slava and me alone. After talking with Mama over lunch, I was prepared to text him about my moving to New York. His being here changes that plan.

"Can we talk?" he asks.

"Sure." I sink into one of the plush reading chairs. "You know you could've just texted or video-called me. You didn't have to fly back just to talk."

"This is a conversation we need to have in person."

"That sounds serious."

"I want to discuss our future."

"Our future?" I ask quietly.

"Svetlana, I loved every second of our time together. I think you did as well."

"I did."

"I don't want this to be the end for us. I want you in my life."

"I'm not sure what to say."

"Say you'll come to Japan with me. We'll figure out where we go from there."

"Slava, I—"

"I'll give you a good life. Much like the one you're used to."

"It's more complicated than that."

"I'm in love with you, Svetlana." His words knock the air from my lungs. "I want to spend forever with you."

"You barely know me." I jump from my chair and walk to the windows to put space between us. "You can't mean that."

Slava follows behind me. "I know everything I need." He turns me to face him. "All you have to do is say yes."

"There's something I haven't told you."

"What is it?"

"I've been accepted at New York University. I'm leaving for the United States in two days."

"I see." He drops his arms. "Why haven't you told me this until now?"

"I didn't think there was reason to. Our dynamic was over, and I had no idea how you felt." My heart sinks with the realization that Mama was right. Even if I didn't think it was important, I should've told him about my plans sooner. Because right now, the look of hurt on his face is almost too much to bear.

"Wow," he says and takes a step back. "I'm not sure what to say." He runs his hands through his hair.

"I'm so sorry. How can I make this right?"

"I don't know that you can."

"Our contract was short-term. Just some fun while you were in town." The words spill from my mouth. "I had no idea you had real feelings for me."

"I told you I wanted more than just a contract with you."

My mind drifts back to his last trip to Moscow. Slava's right. He did tell me, but I blew it off. Or maybe I didn't want to believe what he was saying.

"I think it's time for me to go." He turns his back to me and starts walking out of the room. I can't let him leave like this.

"Slava, wait." I grab his arm. "Let me make this right, please."

"There's nothing you can do right now to fix this. I won't hold you back from New York. I wish you would've told me. Would've allowed me the opportunity to adjust my life to fit your plans."

"You would've gone to New York with me?"

"I would've gone anywhere if it meant I could be with you."

"There's still time. Come with me."

"Svetlana." He cups my cheek in his hand. "You need to find your way, and I deserve to be more than an afterthought."

"Can you ever forgive me?" Tears drip down my face.

"Already done." He leans in, his lips meeting mine.

This kiss is unlike any we've shared before. It's full of

unspoken promises and bittersweet goodbyes. Then, without saying anything, he turns and walks away.

I feel the loss immediately and realize there's no one to blame but myself. The man who may have been my forever has just walked out of my life.

"Slava is gone already?" Papa asks as he enters the room.

"He told me he's in love with me. But I ruined everything."

Papa opens his arms to me, and just like when I was a small child, I cry in the safety of his arms.

"I am sorry that you are hurting," Papa says when my tears subside. "I hope this situation shows you the importance of honesty and communication in a relationship."

"I have." I wipe my cheeks with the back of my hands. "I tried to make it right. I told him I'd like him to come with me, but he said no."

"Moya babochka, your actions hurt Slava deeply. How could you expect him to forget that and move forward?"

"I don't know."

Czarenah was right. I wasn't ready to enter a contract with a Dominant. I wasn't prepared for the depth of the commitment or the level of transparency necessary to make a Dom/sub relationship work. Unfortunately, Slava paid the price for my mistakes. My hope is one day when this pain has passed, he'll give us a second chance.

Svetlana

THE VIEW OF NEW YORK CITY FROM PAPA'S JET IS breathtaking. Although it's night, you'd never know it. The lights from the city's buildings illuminate the sky. It's so different from anything I've seen in Russia.

"I wish I'd come with you before this. I had no idea it was this amazing."

Papa laughs. "We haven't even landed. How do you know you like it?"

"I just have a feeling." I smile. Although the pain from losing Slava is still raw, I also can't quiet the voice inside telling me this adventure will be my best yet.

The plane's wheels slow to a stop, and I unbuckle my safety belt, anxious to take my first steps in the United States.

"After you, little butterfly." Pyotr motions for me to go before him.

As soon as I exit the plane, I'm hit with hot, humid air. It wasn't what I was expecting, especially given the late hour. "I should've worn shorts," I say to Papa, who's waiting at the bottom of the steps.

"Alexander's apartment has air conditioning."

"It's a good thing."

Pyotr joins us as a shiny red Tesla pulls up beside the plane. Alex and Viktor step out of the sleek sports car.

"Max, it's good to see you," Alex greets us as he shakes Papa's hand. "Did you have a good flight?"

"We did," Papa replies before excusing himself to call Mama.

I look around, unsure of what to do next. "Thanks for letting me stay at your apartment. I hope it's not too much of an imposition."

"It's not a problem. I've got plenty of room," Alex reassures me.

"I offered to stay at a hotel, but Papa refused." I sigh loudly.

"He's just looking out for you. It's your first time in the city, and you're a long way from home."

Papa rejoins us. "That was quick."

"She has a busy morning. I caught her in between appointments," Papa replies.

Viktor interrupts, "We're ready to go, boss."

Papa nods. Alex opens the car door. "Let's get going then."

Alex's apartment is supposedly a half hour from the airport. At least, that's what I was told over an hour ago. I've never seen so many cars fill the streets and these crazy yellow taxis that dart in and out of the traffic recklessly.

"If there's this much traffic in the middle of the night, I can't wait to see it during the day," I say sarcastically.

"Traffic is always a guarantee," Viktor says, glancing back at me in the mirror.

"Great." The backseat is not big enough for Alex, Pyotr, and me, making the ride even worse.

"Patience, *moya babochka*," Papa says from the front seat.

After what feels like an eternity, Viktor turns into an underground parking garage. I'm thankful to get out of the car and stretch my legs.

Alex types some numbers on a pad outside the elevator. "I'll make sure you have all the codes to get in and out."

"Thanks." The elevator doors open. "Are you coming, Papa?"

"You two go on ahead. I'll be along shortly."

It's just Alex and me in the elevator. We both fidget nervously, unsure of what to say.

"Are you hungry?" Alex asks.

"A bit, yes."

"I have some takeout menus. You can look through them and pick something to order."

The elevator dings, and the doors open. Alex motions for me to step out before him.

"Is this your apartment?"

"It is."

Everything in the open floor plan is modern and sleek. And we're so high up. Floor-to-ceiling windows offer views of the water and brightly lit buildings.

"Viktor will be up with your bags in a few minutes. In the meantime, I'll show you to your room." Alex leads me down the hall. As we walk, he points out the various rooms we pass. "This one's yours." He opens the door. "I hope you like it."

"It's perfect," I say as I step inside and look around.

"Shall we go order some food?" He looks as nervous as I feel.

"Do you mind if I take a few minutes to freshen up?"

"Sure. Take your time. I'll be in the kitchen when you're ready."

Alex closes the door, leaving me alone. I walk over to the windows that overlook the city. I'm used to looking out and seeing St. Petersburg, where I grew up. Outside this window are modern skyscrapers and streets full of cars—it's a totally foreign sight. The excitement I felt when I stepped off the plane has already disappeared. In its place is anxiousness at just how much my life is about to change.

The reality of what my life is about to be like hits me. After Papa leaves, I'll know exactly three people here. Pyotr, who'll likely be feeling at least some of the anxiety I am since he's also never been to New York City. Viktor, who I don't really get along with. And Alex, the man who's tasked with being my babysitter. He's not a total stranger. He's been around to some degree throughout my childhood. But I don't actually know anything about him. Maybe Papa was right, and I didn't think this through very well because I'm already homesick.

"May I come in," Pyotr calls. I cross the room and open the door. "I've got your stuff."

"Thank you."

"Where do you want them?"

"The bed is fine."

He sets my bags down and studies me for a moment. "You good?"

"I think so. There's going to be a lot to get used to."

"Give yourself some time, little butterfly. Once you become familiar with the city, you'll be okay."

"I'm sure."

"You coming?"

"I'll be out in a few minutes." After freshening up, I find my way back to the kitchen. "Your apartment is lovely," I compliment Alex as I step into the kitchen.

"Sometimes I wonder if I should find something smaller, but the thought of packing and moving isn't appealing." He smiles. "Have a seat. I have the menus here."

"Where's Papa?"

"He's downstairs with Viktor."

"Downstairs?" I ask as I sit on the stool beside him and look through the menus.

"Viktor has an apartment one floor down. They'll be up shortly."

"Is there anything you'd rather?"

"Nope. It's your choice tonight."

I suspect Papa arranged for me to stay with Alex because he's hoping we connect romantically and end up together. Alex is handsome, and he's a Dominant. Those things are attributes in his favor. But he's Alex. He knew me as a child. Saw me wearing braces. Watched me go on my first date and was there when I came home with a broken heart. He's a nice guy, but I see him as more of an older brother.

"How about this one?"

"What do you like on your pizza?"

"I'm a plain kinda girl." Alex raises his eyebrow. "What?"

"Plain?"

"At least for my pizza," I smirk.

Alex

Svetlana's been here for two weeks. Although she says she's doing okay, I get the sense she's struggling. The only thing she's done since she got here is shop. Lana's had poor Pyotr out almost every day. Whatever Maxim pays him isn't enough to compensate for his being dragged around from store to store. Somehow, Pyotr does it without complaining—much.

I'm sure it's difficult trying to acclimate to an entirely different culture. But despite her retail therapy, Lana's not her bubbly, outspoken self. I've been holding off on collaring her. Trying to wait for the perfect time. But perfect doesn't exist, not even for timing. I'll put my collar around her neck this evening, and then we're going to Fire and Ice. It's time to introduce Svetlana to the BDSM community here in NYC.

Me: I'm getting off early tonight. Be ready by 6 to go out.

Lana: Where are we going?

Me: Fire and Ice. I'm on my way into a meeting. I'll text when I'm on my way home.

I was hoping Brandon could go to the club with us tonight, but he hasn't returned home yet. He's been on a business trip in California for the last two weeks. A big tech company is expanding to New York City, and Montgomery Advertising is handling their marketing campaign. Brandon was supposed to have been back a few hours ago, but his flight was canceled because of mechanical issues with the plane. Last I spoke to him, he was still in Denver trying to book a new flight home.

I grab my laptop and head into my conference room, where a group of people is beginning to gather. Once everyone's seated, I motion to two of my newest hires, Ben and Michelle, to start the meeting. They're about to give a presentation to a local client and friend, Ian. He owns a chain of fitness centers and is looking for a creative marketing campaign to increase membership.

While Ben and Michelle give their presentation, I find myself distracted. I'm trying to come up with the best way to give Svetlana my collar of protection later. Several days ago, I spoke to Star, hoping to get some guidance. Other than discussing the importance of what I've agreed to, she had nothing to offer regarding how to collar her. Star said it was entirely up to me, and I'd know what to do when the time was right. I'm beginning to doubt her wisdom because I still have no idea what I'm doing.

Applause draws my attention back to the room.

"I'm impressed with what you've come up with," Ian says. "It's almost as though you were in my head."

"We're delighted you like it," Michelle responds with a smile.

"You have some rising stars here, Alex."

"I think you're right."

Ian spends a few minutes sharing his ideas on how to fine-tune the ads before walking out with Michelle and Beb.

Me: I'll be ready to go in about 15 minutes.

Viktor: The car will be out front waiting for you.

I need a few minutes alone to put my thoughts together.

I texted Lana that I was on my way home, but she didn't text back. I've tried calling twice, but I keep getting her voicemail. My mood goes from bad to worse when the elevator doors open, and I'm assaulted with music so loud I'm surprised the windows aren't shaking. I drop my stuff on the table and pull my phone out to shut the music off.

"Who turned my music off?" The last word is cut short when a towel-clad Lana nearly collides with me.

"I did."

Her hand flies up to her chest. "Holy shit, Alex. I didn't hear you come in."

"How could you with the music up so loud." I cross my arms. "I tried texting and calling you."

"You did?" She looks at her phone. "Obviously, I didn't hear that either."

"You have ten minutes to be dressed and in the living room. We need to talk."

I turn to leave before I explode.

"Great. I'm with another bossy man."

"I heard that," I call over my shoulder.

"And?" she yells back.

I freeze midstep. Part of me wants to turn around and put her over my knee for disrespecting me. The other part knows we have no formal agreement. I choose not to engage her any further for fear that I'll choose option one. Instead, I go to my bedroom to get changed.

I'm sitting on the sofa waiting for Lana. She has thirty seconds before she's late, and I cancel tonight. With five seconds to spare, she hurries into the room.

"You're lucky. Your time was almost up."

"Fifteen minutes was barely enough time to blow-dry my hair."

"If you didn't have the music on so loud, you would've known when I was coming home. That won't happen again, will it?"

"No."

"Sit." She lowers herself onto the cushion at the far end of the couch. Here goes nothing. "You are well aware that your father asked me to serve as your protector Dominant."

"About that. I don't think it's necessary, do you?"

This girl isn't for real. "Maxim told me you agreed. Is that not true?"

"Well, I kinda agreed."

I sit back and motion for her to keep talking.

"I didn't want to say yes, but it was one of Papa's stipulations before he agreed to allow me to come to New York. So, I said yes, but figured you and I could work out something else once I was here."

"Absolutely not. I promised your father I would do this. Unlike you, giving my word means something to me." The smile she was wearing disappears. "So, you have a choice to make. Either you will follow through on your word and wear my collar of protection, or we'll call your father and see how he wants to proceed."

"You'd do that?"

"Yes."

"Fine." She crosses her arms. "I guess we'll do this your way."

"Svetlana, I'm not your enemy."

Svetlana

"I'M SICK OF BEING TOLD WHAT TO DO. IT MAKES ME feel like a child."

"My role as your protector isn't to boss you around. It's to ensure your safety. You're in an unfamiliar place, and you're going to meet a lot of people you don't know. I can guarantee men at the club will be interested in you."

"You think I can't handle myself?"

"In my opinion, I don't think you're prepared for that."

"I've had a Dominant before." I know I sound like a petulant child, but I can't help it. Alex is driving me crazy already.

"And how did that go?"

"It was really good. Until it wasn't."

"Can I ask what happened?" Alex softens his voice.

"I screwed up." I get choked up thinking about the look on Slava's face before he left. "I kept things from him and ended up hurting him." I'm waiting for the lecture that I'm sure will come, but what Alex does next surprises me.

"I've made some pretty bad decisions in my past, too. Before my mom passed away, I had a submissive. We'd been together for a little over a year. I really cared about her. After my mom died, I

spiraled out of control and left her without so much as an explanation." He runs a hand through his hair. "I hurt her badly. It
took time for me to see how my actions affected her and to make
it right."

"How did you fix it?"

"I didn't say I fixed it. I said I made it right. There's a
difference."

"Did you ask her for a second chance?"

"No."

"Why not?"

"Because even though she forgave me, she didn't want me in
her life." My heart sinks. "It was hard to accept, but I had no one
to blame other than myself."

"Things are different with Slava and me."

"If you keep trying when he already said no, he's only going to
see that as disrespect," Alex says softly. "You need to accept that
you messed up, and that door's closed."

"If I don't keep trying, he'll think I gave up. That I don't
care."

"Knowing when to walk away isn't easy. But if you really care
about Slava, you'll respect his wishes."

I don't like what Alex is saying. It's not what I want to hear. "I
never meant to hurt him."

"Making mistakes is part of being human. But it's important
to learn from your experience and not repeat it."

"I guess."

Alex smiles. "Now, back to the matter at hand. The collar."
He grabs a small box from the table. "Are you ready to move
forward?"

"Yes. Do I have to call you sir?"

"No. Alex will be fine," he chuckles. "I do have some expectations, though."

"What are they?" I roll my eyes, certain he'll have a long list
for me to follow.

"While you're staying here, I'm going to ask that you're respectful. Playing music is fine. Blasting it is not."

"I'm sorry. It won't happen again."

"I forgive you. I also need to know that you'll respect my place as your protector. When we're at the club, you will not approach a Dominant or do anything behind my back."

"What if there's someone I'm interested in? I can't talk to them?"

"Not unless it's cleared through me."

I was right. He's just another person who wants to tell me what I can and can't do. "I can take care of myself."

"I'm sure you can." Alex sighs loudly. "But for now, you don't have to. I'm assuming that responsibility for you. I'm not trying to limit you or hold you back."

"Then, I guess I don't understand."

"My goal is to ensure your safety and, hopefully, your happiness. I want to get to know you as more than Maxim's kid. I want to know who Svetlana is. This way, I'll have an easier time pre-vetting Dominants for you. I want you to enjoy this transitional time."

His explanation sounds reasonable. "Okay. I won't approach any Dominants without your consent."

"I hope you like it." He lifts the collar, which is more like a delicate necklace, from the box. "I wanted it to be something you could wear without attracting unwanted attention. What you choose to tell others is up to you."

I examine the silver chain, the pendant with his initials, and the lowercase *p*. It's something only people in our lifestyle would recognize. It's clear he put a lot of thought into this. That's evidenced by the garnet that dangles under the charm. "It's beautiful." I turn around and hold my hair up so Alex can put the collar on.

"I promise I'll do my best to be understanding and fair. And to keep the lines of communication between us open," Alex says as he does the clasp.

"I promise to do my best to submit to and respect your guidance."

"Are you ready to go to Fire and Ice?"

Svetlana

HOMESICK. THAT'S A WORD I NEVER THOUGHT WOULD come out of my mouth. But I'm terribly homesick. I've spoken to my parents several times since moving. Papa's main concern is that I'm not going out without Pyotr. He's always focused on my safety first. Mama asks how I'm adjusting and if I've started making friends. She realizes the challenge of living with three men. I've gotten good at giving my parents a polished speech to reassure them I love living in a big modern city. The time difference makes having lengthy conversations tricky. Something I'm not complaining about. If our phone calls went any longer, I'm sure they'd see through my story. Because the reality is, I'm doubting everything.

New York is unlike anything I've ever experienced. I'd read it's called the city that never sleeps, but until I got here, I didn't realize how literal that statement is. It's like there's a power switch that's always turned on.

The first few days, I was mesmerized by the fast pace and the convenience of having anything I could dream of available at all times. Shopping was just as good, if not better than the stories I'd heard. For the first few weeks, I dragged Pyotr out almost every day to add to my wardrobe and buy more things I didn't need for my dorm. But that got old fast. The constant go, go, go that is Manhattan is exhausting. I find myself longing for the quiet seclusion of our home in St. Petersburg.

I think the worst part of all this is that I'm lonely. The only people I know here are the men I live with. Until school starts in September, meeting people is going to be difficult. Pyotr is just as unfamiliar with the city as I am. The difference is I'm okay with exploring, but Pyotr insists we stay in the small area Alex and Viktor told him is safe. Viktor promised to take Pyotr out and show him more of the city so we could branch out, but that hasn't happened yet. Alex works a lot, so Viktor's always gone. I'm hoping tonight signals a change in all that. Alex is finally taking me to Fire and Ice.

My fingers go to the collar around my neck. I'm still not entirely comfortable with it. I knew Alex had made an agreement with Papa. I didn't anticipate that he would expect me to follow through with it. I mean, why would he want to be tied to a girl he barely knows? Unless he's thinking that I'm going to fall for him. There's no chance of that ever happening. Alexander Montgomery may be handsome, but he is definitely not my type.

Viktor pulls the car up to the curb. "Is there a particular time you want to be picked up?"

"I'm not sure yet. I'll text you later."

"No problem. Have a good evening."

Viktor jumps out and gets my door. "Thanks, Vik."

"Have fun."

"But not too much fun, little butterfly," Pyotr calls from the front seat.

"Aren't you coming?"

"Nope. Viktor's taking me out for the tour he promised."

"I guess I'll see you later." As much as I complain about always having Pyotr with me, I already miss his presence. It feels foreign being without him.

"You ready?" Alex asks.

"I think so." I try to maintain a calm exterior, but inside I'm freaking out. "Do I look okay?"

"I would've preferred you wear something a bit more substantial."

"For real?" It took me forever to pick out an outfit earlier. Finally, I settled on a red bodycon dress with a cutout mid-drift and a pair of black Louboutin heels I bought the other day. It's a sexy choice that I'm sure will draw some attention my way. "Don't women here wear similar clothes?"

"They do."

"Then, what's the problem?"

"I'm going to have my hands full with the men and women who'll be inquiring about you. I won't be able to enjoy my evening." He laughs.

I roll my eyes. "Very funny."

"Come on." He places his hand on my back. "Let's go in."

My first impression is that of confusion. We're standing in a lobby with no indication that this is a club. If not for the discreet sign indicating bracelet colors and meanings, I'd question if we're in the right place.

"Good evening, Alex."

"Good evening, Star. I want to introduce you to Svetlana Solonik."

"It's a pleasure to meet you," the woman says. "I've heard so much about you from your father."

"It's good to meet you as well."

"How are you finding our city so far?"

"I haven't gotten to see much of it yet."

"I've been swamped at work," Alex explains. "I'm afraid I haven't been the best host."

"Shame on you, Alexander," she says, half joking. Alex shrugs. "May I steal your submissive for a few minutes? I promise to return her in one piece."

"Sure. I'll be inside."

Alex pulls open one of the tall wooden doors, and I quickly glance inside to what must be the main room.

"Let me text Owen so he can cover the desk, and then I'll give you the grand tour." She swipes at her phone screen. "He'll be out in a minute. In the meantime, let me explain our color levels."

After I'm given a purple bracelet, the color indicating not to approach me directly, we set off on our tour.

The club's main room is brightly lit and has a modern warehouse vibe. It's very different than Ecstasy and Noire, but I like it. Music plays in the background but is not so loud that you can't hear the person next to you.

Although I don't recognize faces, I see familiarity in the people around me. For the first time since I got here, I feel at home.

"As you can see, we have three stages for members who wish to do public scenes." Two of the stages are set up, but nothing is happening at the current moment. "We have a café if you get hungry while you're here."

"Whatever they're cooking in there smells incredible."

"It's a popular spot for club members." Star leads me to a hall. "These are our private rooms. They're all in use, or I'd give you a tour."

"Are they all the same?"

"The rooms at the end of the hall are our themed rooms." She motions to the doors that are closer. "These are the aftercare rooms. They're done in more muted tones. I'm sure Alex will show them to you when they're not occupied. Do you have any other questions?"

"Not right now."

"Then, I'll return you to your Dominant. He's probably wondering where you are."

"I'm sure Alex wouldn't mind if you kept me all night."

"I doubt that."

"He's not very happy to have me with him."

"What gives you that impression?" she asks with genuine interest.

"I don't know. I just have a feeling."

"Alex is a complicated man. But he's kind and fair. I promise you're in good hands."

"I'll try."

We search the club for Alex and find him in the far corner, speaking with several people. As we approach, all heads turn my way.

"Looks like you're attracting attention already," Star whispers.

"I'm sure Alex is going to love that."

"Give him a chance before you make a judgment."

Although Alex isn't a total stranger, I really don't know him. I knew he was in the lifestyle, but I've never been privy to this part of his life. Because of our age difference, we were never more than acquaintances. Whenever he was at our house, I was just the kid he had to be nice to because I was the boss's daughter. Being roommates who are in this Dom/sub protective relationship is uncharted territory for both of us.

"Did you enjoy your tour?" Alex asks when Star walks away.

"I did," I answer without looking at him. Instead, I'm checking out the guys Alex has been talking to. One, in particular, is drool-worthy. "Are you going to introduce me to your friends?"

"No."

"Seriously?" I cross my arms. "I can't believe this."

"If you men will excuse us, I need to speak to my submissive privately." Alex wastes no time taking my hand and leading me away.

I pull out of his grasp. "You didn't have plans to introduce me to anyone tonight, did you?"

"I'm not discussing this right here. Come with me." He doesn't stop walking until he finds who he's apparently looking for. "May I use your office for a few minutes, Star?"

"Sure." She looks between us. "Is everything okay?"

"No."

"Come with me. I'll unlock it for you."

"Let's go." Alex's tone is icy.

We follow Star down the hall with the private rooms and turn the corner. This is part of the club that wasn't included in my earlier tour. Mistress Star swipes a card, and the lock clicks open. Alex enters her office, but I don't move.

"Are you just going to stand there?"

"Maybe."

"I think inside the office is a more appropriate place to sort out whatever this is," Star suggests. I follow the Domme into her office.

"I cannot believe you behaved that way in front of those men. You do realize they were Dominants?"

"How would I know that? You didn't bother to introduce me."

"There was no reason to."

"Isn't that the point of all this?" I wave my hand around.

"The point is that you need someone to look out for you because clearly, you're too immature to do it for yourself."

"Okay, you two." Star intervenes. "Take a seat, and we'll discuss this calmly." After we sit, Star asks Alex what happened, and then she turns to me for my take. She listens attentively to both our sides. "Svetlana, I'm going to have to agree with Alex on this. That kind of behavior from a submissive is disrespectful."

"How will I meet anyone if *he* refuses to introduce me?"

"When and who I choose to introduce you to is up to me," Alex interrupts.

"I knew this was a mistake. You probably have no intention of letting me meet anyone."

"Svetlana, that'll be enough," Star says sternly. "Remember that you are a submissive."

"Isn't his job to help me meet a Dominant?"

"That's part of his job, yes. But it will not happen on your terms. This is only your first night here. There's no reason to jump into meeting a Dominant."

"But—" Star holds up her hand, silencing me.

"It's more important for you to acclimate to Fire and Ice and meet other submissives. Becoming part of our community is an important step in your journey. You must trust that Alex will introduce you to the Dominants when he feels the time is right."

"And if he never thinks it's the right time?"

"If you keep acting like this, there won't be—" This time, Star interrupts Alex.

"Did you discuss your expectations for this dynamic before you came here?"

"Yes," we both answer.

"Alex, did you explain how you'll handle any introductions to Svetlana."

"I did."

"And did you agree to respect Alex's dominance in this relationship?"

"I did."

"I've worked hard to develop high standards for both the Dominants and submissives who come to my club. Alex is a respected member of this community, and I don't doubt he's acting with your best interest in mind. If I see him, or anyone else, out of line, I don't hesitate to step in. Your dynamic is no different. Do you understand?"

"I do. I'm sorry for being rude." I look to Alex. "This move hasn't been easy for me."

"I know that, and I apologize for being largely unavailable the past few weeks. Work needed to take priority. I wasn't going to tell you yet, but I'll be off all next week. I planned to take you out to show you more of the city."

"Really?"

"Yes, really." He lets out a frustrated breath. "I need you to trust me."

"I understand."

"Are we okay now?" Star asks.

Alex looks at me, and I nod. "We're good," he says.

"You two go on ahead. I have a few things to do in here."

On the way back to the main room, I notice one of the private rooms is no longer in use. "These were all occupied earlier. Star suggested I ask you to show me one when they were free."

"Sure." He swipes his card and opens the door.

It's as if I've stepped into another realm. "It's a dungeon."

"It is." Alex stays in the doorway while I walk around.

"This room is incredible." The faux stone that covers the walls looks and feels authentic. On the ceiling are wooden beams that only add to the dark aesthetics. Electric candles provide dim lighting. This room has everything from a St. Catherine's Wheel to a stockade. Chains hang from the ceiling for bondage and suspension. There's even a throne. "I'd love to play in here."

"Duly noted."

"I take it you don't like torture and pain?"

"It's not my thing."

"You don't know what you're missing out on."

A couple appears in the doorway.

"Hey, Alex," a woman says. "Did we have the wrong time?"

"No." He motions to me. "I was letting Lana take a look around."

"Did you get a new sub?"

"Not exactly. Lana, I'd like to introduce you to Kate and her submissive, Raul."

"It's a pleasure to meet you," I say and keep my gaze down.

"You as well."

"We'll get out of your way. It was nice seeing you." I follow Alex down the hall. "I'm impressed. You can behave."

Over the course of the night, Alex introduced me to several submissives. We exchanged numbers so we could keep in touch. Alex chose not to introduce me to any Dominants. I hoped he'd change his mind, but he didn't. Although the evening got off to a rocky start, it ended on a much better note. It's the early hours of the morning when we exit the club. Viktor and Pyotr are waiting outside next to the car.

"Are you an expert on the city now?" I ask Pyotr.

"I have a much better feel for it. How was your evening?"

"I had a great time."

"I hope she wasn't too much of a handful?" Pyotr asks jokingly.

"She could use to be bent over someone's knee."

"As if."

"Come on, let's get you home."

I'm quiet on the ride back to Alex's apartment. Alex asked me to trust him, but I behaved like an entitled brat instead. I drop my head back onto the seat. Screwing up seems to be my lot in life, and to be honest, I don't know how to change it.

Brandon

"Hey." I pop my head into Alex's office. "How was the rest of your weekend?"

"Less eventful than Friday night." I got back into town about three a.m. on Saturday and called Alex. I'm glad I called because he needed to discuss what happened between him and Lana at the club. "Come on in."

"I only have a few minutes," I say as I close the door.

"I don't know what I'm doing," Alex confesses.

"What do you mean?"

"Lana spent the rest of the weekend in her room. She barely said two words to me." He runs his hands through his hair. "Do you think I was too hard on her?"

"From what you described, no. She overstepped, and you corrected her. It's a necessary part of any Dom/sub dynamic."

"That part was always hard for me. I guess I thought it would be easier not being in an actual relationship. I was wrong."

"She'll eventually meet someone, and your work will be done."

"I don't know anyone who's looking for a sub that's as challenging as Lana's going to be. She's very—" Alex hesitates. "—Spirited."

The alarm on my cell goes off. "Sorry. I have a video conference in five minutes."

"Do you have plans tonight?"

"No. What's up?"

"Why don't you come over. We'll grab some takeout, and you can meet Svetlana."

"Sure. From what it sounds like, this might be a good show. I'll make sure to bring some popcorn."

"You're a regular comedian, Carpenter."

"I called Tony for dinner," Alex says as we take the elevator to the ground floor. "We have to stop by the restaurant on the way home."

Tony's been a regular at Fire and Ice since the club opened over twenty years ago. He's a master with wax and often does scenes with his sub, Leo, showcasing his talent. But his mastery doesn't end there. He also owns what I think is the best restaurant in the city, Italiano Desiderio. "I'll never say no to his food."

"Me either. I was glad he squeezed in a takeout order on such short notice."

Viktor double parks outside the restaurant while Alex runs in to grab the food.

"What do you think of Svetlana?" I ask Viktor.

Viktor glances at me through the rearview mirror. "Lana might come off as rebellious and indifferent at first, but I suspect it's just her way of guarding herself. Her sister's abduction was traumatizing for her. I suspect she's never fully processed that. It's easy to overlook that aspect of her when you're around her." His observation is intriguing. I've never heard anyone describe her like that before. "She's certainly giving Alex a run for his money," Viktor adds, grinning.

"I've heard."

Alex and Tony walk toward the car, their hands full. Viktor jumps out and grabs the bags from Tony. He gives a small wave and hurries back into his restaurant.

"Tony apologized he couldn't stay and talk," Alex says as he slides into the back seat. "He's got a packed house."

"It looks like he made enough for an army." There are five bags filled to the top with food that smells delicious.

"He went over and above as usual."

As we finish the drive to Montgomery's apartment, Viktor's insights about Svetlana linger in my mind. His depiction casts a fresh perspective on the girl I've only heard about. I find myself intrigued and eager to meet her.

"You ready for this?" Alex asks as we exit the car and grab the bags.

"Of course."

"I don't know what Lana or the apartment will be like when we get up there."

"I'm sure it'll be fine."

It's a short trip to his penthouse apartment. The elevator doors open, and his place is quiet as usual.

"I don't know what's worse. Walking in here with the music blasting or complete silence?" We set the bags on the island in his kitchen. "I'll go find Lana."

While he searches for his houseguest, I get the food out of the bag and grab place settings for us.

He returns a few minutes later. "She'll be out shortly."

We're just sitting down to eat when she enters the room. I look up to find the most beautiful woman walking on planet Earth. I'm immediately drawn to her eyes, which are a striking shade of sapphire. They're unlike anything I've ever seen. Her chestnut brown hair with hints of caramel and honey hangs long down her back. I envision it wrapped around my hand while I'm driving into her.

Alex clears his throat. "Svetlana, this is my good friend, Brandon. Brandon, this is Maxim's daughter, Svetlana."

"It's nice to meet you," she says.

"You as well. I've heard a lot about you."

"You have?" She looks at Alex.

"Brandon's a Dominant at the club."

"Is that how you two know each other?"

"That's how we met. But now we also work together," Alex explains. "Brandon's aware of your father's involvement in my company."

Lana's the picture of submission throughout the rest of dinner. She's polite and only answers when spoken to. There's no sign of the stubborn, outspoken girl I've heard everyone describe her as. I'm starting to think Viktor's assessment of her is more accurate than he realizes.

Svetlana

ALEX: I'VE INVITED A FRIEND FOR DINNER. PLEASE BE on your best behavior.

Me: I'm not a child.

Delete

Me: Really, Alex? You sound like Papa.

Delete

I go through several more texts that I delete without sending. I want to do the right thing, but I'm not sure what that is.

Me: I've made a mess of things and could really use someone to talk to.

I hit send, and then I wait. It's over an hour when my phone finally rings.

"Hello?"

"I got your text."

"Thank you for calling."

"I'm glad you reached out."

This is harder than I thought it would be. "I screwed up and ruined everything."

"Want to tell me what's going on?" Masha asks.

I take a few minutes to fill her in on my last interaction with Slava as well as everything that's occurred since I got here.

"Do you remember what we talked about before you left? That there'll be setbacks."

"I remember. But this is more than a setback."

"We all make mistakes. The important thing is that we learn from them."

I've only learned that I have a special talent for hurting the people around me. "Masha, I need your help. I embarrassed myself, but I don't care about that. What I care about is that I made Alex look bad. And now I don't know how to face him again."

"You know I'm not a part of that lifestyle. However, it sounds like his reaction was fair."

"I didn't like it, but it was fair."

"Is he still holding it over your head, or has he put it behind him?"

"He didn't say a word about it after we stepped out of Mistress Star's office."

"So, what's your plan for moving forward?"

"I have to respect him and not be so outspoken."

"You're very good at giving the expected answers."

"What do you mean?"

"Svetlana, ever since I met you, you've been the perfect patient. You answer each question with what you *think* is the correct answer. What I'm hoping to hear."

"Isn't that what you want?"

"No."

"I don't understand."

"I want to hear what you really think. What you really feel. I need to know what's underneath the mask. The stuff you don't let others see."

Although that's not the response I was expecting, I recognize this is a pivotal moment. If I don't lay everything out in the open, I may lose this chance and never experience the growth I need to become a proper submissive.

"You're right. I've become quite good at playing the game. But I'm done. I'm so tired and can't do it anymore."

"Is that all?"

"I'm scared." Tears begin to fall. "I'm terrified to give up control."

"That's what I've been waiting for you to admit for so long." She softens her voice.

We discuss how my sister's abduction and the helplessness I felt watching her being taken away. She's right. Even though I went to therapy while I was in Moscow, I never allowed her past my protective exterior—never dealt with the trauma I've carried around my entire life.

"When you meet the right Dominant, your submission will be a true gift. One that you'll freely give."

"I already met him."

"Have you met someone since arriving in the United States?"

"No. It's Slava. He's the one."

"Is he?"

"Yes, I'm certain of it."

"Before you say anything else, I need you to hear me out, okay?"

"Okay."

"Slava swept you off your feet. You were attracted to him both in looks and the knowledge that he's solid and settled. You had fun with him. But the entire time you were together, it was on your terms. Is that an accurate description?"

"I agreed to weekends only and that the contract would end when my school term finished. Was I wrong to have asked for those things?"

"From my understanding, there's no clear right or wrong during negotiations. It's something unique to each couple. Much like any *vanilla* relationship, the important part is that both members feel heard and have come to an agreement."

"We did."

"Yes, you did. But from the outside looking in, it appears you set the boundaries, and Slava did the compromising. He asked one thing of you, to discuss a more committed relationship after school. When the time came, you refused to do that. You went so far as to withhold information from him that directly affected that."

"Yes, but—"

"It doesn't matter what kind of a relationship you're in. Complete honesty is essential. Didn't I stress that when we spoke?"

"You did."

"Why do you think you weren't honest with him?"

"That's a complicated answer."

"I'm okay with complicated," Masha chuckles.

"Slava's everything any submissive would want in a Dominant. Heck, he's everything any woman could ever wish for in a man. And the time we spent together was phenomenal." I smile at the memories. "But every time I thought about being with him long term, I felt like I'd be giving up a part of me that I was unwilling to sacrifice."

"Can you explain that further?"

"Slava's so settled. I assumed he was looking for a submissive who would be willing to slide into his already perfect life. But I wasn't ready to do that. I still had dreams and goals for my future that I thought I'd be giving up if I stayed with him. I didn't tell him because I feared he'd reject me. It was easier for me to reject him and blame it on circumstances."

"That's an excellent observation."

"I was wrong, though. I didn't know that Slava would've changed his life for me. And because I wasn't honest, he was hurt. But I'm going to make it right and get him back."

"Did he offer you that option?"

"Not exactly."

"Not exactly?"

"No, he didn't."

"Svetlana, you need to respect his decision to walk away. When you meet the right Dominant for you, submitting to him won't feel like you're giving up who you are to be in their life. You'll grow as a person and as a couple. Your past, present, *and* future will make sense, and you won't fear losing yourself. Slava's a good man, but he was not the right one for you."

"If I was honest, like everyone told me, things would be so different. I'd still have Slava."

"That's not a guarantee. We can't go back in time and ask for a do-over. What's done is done."

"What do I do now?"

"First, you need to stop hyper-focusing on the past." Sometimes her keen observations scare me. "I've said this before, and I'll say it again, you must start looking at the bigger picture."

By the time we hang up, I feel I have a better handle on myself and what I need to do from now on.

Me: Thank you for letting me know. I'll do my best.

Alex: I appreciate that.

I'm reading a book when there's a knock on my door. "Come in."

"It's just me. I wanted to let you know I'm home and brought dinner."

"Okay. I'll be out in a minute."

"Right." He looks puzzled, but he doesn't say anything else.

After he leaves, I put my book away and give myself a once over in the mirror. I don't know who Alex has brought home, but I want to ensure I'm presentable.

When I get to the kitchen, Alex is sitting at the table with another man who turns when he hears me enter the room. His dark eyes are soft and gentle. I'm momentarily captivated by his intense gaze.

Alex clears his throat, breaking whatever spell I'm under. "Svetlana, this is my good friend, Brandon. Brandon, this is Maxim's daughter, Svetlana."

"It's nice to meet you," I say and sit in my usual chair.

"You as well. I've heard a lot about you."

"You have?" I look at Alex.

"Brandon's a Dominant at the club."

"Is that how you two know each other?"

"That's how we met. But now we also work together," Alex explains. "Brandon's aware of your father's involvement in my company."

While we eat, Brandon and Alex discuss some upcoming projects at work. I eat silently, avoiding any intrusion into their conversation. It isn't until they begin talking about a Fire and Ice event and whether either of them has plans to attend this weekend that I take notice. Apparently, a Dominant named Anthony is doing a sensual wax scene with his submissive, Leopold.

After polishing off the massive portion of chicken parmesan and pasta on my plate, I make a mental note to ask Alex the name of the restaurant. It's the most exquisite Italian food I've ever tasted.

As soon as everyone has finished eating, I rise from my seat. Alex looks at me with uncertainty about my next move.

"May I take your plate, Sir?"

"You may. And you don't need to call me Sir."

"I didn't want to be rude in front of your guest."

"I appreciate that, but Alex is fine no matter who's around."

"Thank you." I turn to Brandon. "May I take your plate?"

"Sure. Thanks." He smiles.

"You can leave that stuff in the sink. We'll take care of it later." Alex says as he and Brandon move to the living room.

I struggle with what I should do. Do I go ahead and wash the dishes or leave them in the sink? I settle with following Alex's instructions and leave everything for later. Then, I walk toward the hall leading to my room.

"You're more than welcome to hang out with us," Alex says, stopping me mid-step.

"I don't want to intrude."

"Don't be silly."

I sit in the extra wide chair across from the couch the guys are on and tuck my feet under my legs.

"Alex tells me you'll be attending NYU in the fall."

"I am."

"What are you studying?"

"Political science."

"Nice. What do you want to do with that degree."

"I hope it will help me get accepted to law school."

"That's terrific. Will you be staying in New York for your graduate degree?"

"That's my plan. If everything works out, I'd like to stay here permanently."

Alex's cell rings. He checks the screen. "If you two will excuse me, I need to take this."

"How are you finding New York so far?" Brandon asks.

"It's an incredible city. Although it can be a bit overwhelming at times."

"That's an understatement."

"Have you lived here for long?" I ask.

"I was born and raised in Brooklyn."

"And you still find it overwhelming?"

"I do. That's why I keep my house in Brooklyn. Sometimes, I need a break from the craziness of Manhattan." The conversation comes to an awkward pause. "Are you coming to the club with Alex this weekend?"

"I don't know. Alex hasn't said anything about it."

"Right. I hope he decides to bring you. The things Anthony does with wax are amazing."

"Sorry about that." Alex comes back into the room. "Looks like I'm going to have to go into work on Monday after all."

"Maxim?" Brandon asks.

This time, it's my phone that rings. "It's Papa."

"Go on and answer it."

"It was nice meeting you, Brandon." I smile.

"You, too."

I leave the guys in the living room to talk to my parents.

Brandon

Since meeting Svetlana earlier this week, I haven't been able to get her out of my head. During our meal, there was a palpable tension between her and Alex. I know he was worried about how she'd act. She maintained her polite demeanor, but I could sense the fiery nature that people often attribute to her just beneath the surface. I want to see her again and get to know her better, but I'm uncertain how to broach the subject.

"Got a minute?" Alex asks from my doorway.

"Sure."

His movements are stiff as he closes the door and sits across from my desk.

"Is everything okay?" I take my glasses off and set them on the desk.

Alex takes a deep breath. "When are you going to ask about Lana?"

"What?"

He leans forward. "You've asked me about her every day for the past month."

"I have?" Here I thought I was being subtle. I guess not.

"You have. When are you going to take the next step?"

"I have been uncertain about what to say and when to say it." After the rough start she and Alex got off to, he wanted to make sure all that was in her past before he moved forward with pre-vetting Dominants for her. The three of us have spent some time together, and all my interactions with Lana have been positive. She appears to have adjusted and is in a better state than before. Although she still challenges Alex, she does so privately, which is more appropriate. A submissive always has a voice. It seems she needed practice using it effectively. "I would like your permission to pursue Svetlana."

"You have my blessing."

"How do you think she's going to feel about this?"

"I don't guess anything when it comes to Svetlana." He holds his hands up. "The best way to find out is to ask her. Why don't you come over tonight? I can find something to keep myself busy while you two talk."

"Thanks, Montgomery."

"I have some real work to get to now."

After he leaves the office, I lean back in my chair. It's been a long time since I've pursued a submissive, and I've never been interested in someone as complicated as Lana. She's younger than anyone I've considered. Even though she was raised in this lifestyle, she doesn't have a lot of personal experience. And I can't overlook her sometimes unpredictable nature. Then, there are the demons I've yet to face. I'll have to proceed cautiously so that neither of us gets in over our heads.

When the elevator doors open to Alex's apartment, we're hit with the smell of something mouthwatering coming from the kitchen.

"She cooks, too? You've been holding out on me, Montgomery."

"I had no idea, but I guess we're not ordering out," he says as we enter the kitchen, where we find Svetlana at the stove. "What are you making?"

"Beef Stroganoff," she says as she turns around. "Brandon, I didn't know you were coming over tonight."

"I hope you don't mind."

"Not at all. I made more than enough." She looks at Alex. "I hope you don't mind. I invited Viktor and Pyotr for dinner. This is Pyotr's favorite meal."

"Actually, I'm going to need to steal them for a bit. There's something important we have to take care of. Do you mind entertaining Brandon for me? We'll grab leftovers later."

"Umm. Sure, if that's what you want."

"Thanks." Clasping my shoulder, he says quietly, "Good luck." Then, he disappears.

"Is there anything I can help with?"

"Dinner will be ready in a second. I have a bottle of Barolo chilling. Would you mind opening it?"

"Not at all."

I've spent enough time at Montgomery's place to know where everything is. I grab the corkscrew and find the bottle she mentioned. While I pour the wine, Lana makes our plates.

"I hope you like it."

She watches me intently as I take my first bite. "Wow. This is incredible."

"Thank you." She blushes.

"Where did you learn to cook like this?"

"Mama and Olga."

"Is Olga your grandmother?"

"No, Olga is our cook."

"They obviously passed their talent to you."

"I'm afraid it wasn't that simple. Being in the kitchen was of very little interest to me. In my country, women need to be able to cook. So, I was forced to learn."

"If this meal is an indication, I'd say you learned well."

"It took a while. Poor Papa was subjected to some very questionable meals," she giggles. "Fortunately, I've improved since then and have grown to enjoy being in the kitchen."

We eat silently for a few minutes, but it's not awkward. On the contrary, it's comfortable. As if we've done this many times.

"Alex tells me you're getting ready to move out. You must be excited."

"Actually, I'm terrified," she confesses. "I don't know what uni will be like here compared to Moscow. And what if my roommate hates me?"

"I don't have experience with college, so I won't be much help with that. But I don't think there's any way your roommate could hate you."

"You didn't go to college?"

"No. My parents were older when they had me. By the time I graduated from high school, they needed extra help. So, instead of attending college, I got a job and cared for them."

"That's a very selfless thing to do. They must appreciate the sacrifice you made."

"They did. They're both gone now."

"I had no idea. I'm very sorry."

"It was a tough loss, but I'm learning how to live with it."

"I understand loss. Obviously, you know about my sister."

"I do. I can't imagine how difficult that was for you."

"I still have nightmares about it sometimes." She sets her fork down and takes a sip of her wine. "People always say that the pain gets better or goes away, but it doesn't. It's always there. If not at the forefront of my mind, it's just below the surface. Somedays, it feels like it was just yesterday she was taken, and other days, I struggle to remember what she looked like—what her voice sounded like."

"I know what you mean. I don't believe grief goes away. We learn how to live in spite of it."

"That's exactly it. Not many people understand that."

"I think they do. Whether we like it or not, we're going to lose people we love. The problem is that because grief and loss are uncomfortable, people try to sweep it under the rug and pretend it doesn't happen. Then, we're taught to give these pretty answers that supposedly make people feel better."

"You may be right. I know I've tried to do that myself. But pretending it hasn't happened or because it's been so many years, everything is suddenly okay doesn't work."

"You're not the only one who's tried that." Lana gets up to clear our now empty plates. I follow her into the kitchen. "Can I help you with the dishes?"

"There's no need. I can do them."

"I know you can, but I'd like to help."

"If you really want to."

If she only knew what I really wanted to do with her. But I can't jump right to that. I need to keep my body under control and take this one step at a time. I've made mistakes in the past. Skipped necessary steps with a submissive, and the results were disastrous. I don't want to do that with Svetlana.

There's something different about her. About the way I feel when I'm near her.

Svetlana

I'M CAUGHT OFF GUARD WHEN ALEX SAYS HE WON'T BE here for dinner. He tries to be around in the evenings, especially for dinner. But I know sometimes Papa calls with an emergency that needs to be addressed immediately. Usually, Pyotr stays with me, though. Knowing Alex needs both men is concerning. I want to call Papa and find out what's going on. But Alex asked me to entertain Brandon, and I don't want to be rude.

While Brandon pours the wine, I prepare myself for an uncomfortable dinner. Every time we hung out, Alex was there too. Brandon seems like a nice guy, but I really don't know anything about him and have no idea what to talk about. That situation is quickly resolved when we start talking about our families. Brandon's experienced a great deal of loss, as well.

Now, he's helping me do the dishes. It feels oddly familiar. We work side-by-side as though we've done this routine many times before.

"Would you like to go for a walk?" Brandon asks as I'm putting the last dish away.

"Sure. But I need to ask Alex first."

"Not a problem."

I take out my phone to send a text.

Me: Brandon asked me to go for a walk. Is that okay with you?

It's a few minutes before the bubbles begin dancing on my screen, indicating Alex is typing.

Alex: Is that something you'd like to do?

Me: Yes.

Alex: It's fine with me. Have fun.

"He said yes."

Brandon's face lights up. "Great. Let's go."

We're quiet on the elevator ride down to the ground floor. When the doors open, Pyotr is waiting at the building's entrance.

"And here I thought I'd get to go out without an escort."

"It's fine. I don't mind," Brandon says and smiles.

"I'm glad *you* don't. Nobody ever asks me if I mind."

"Your safety is important."

"Are you saying you wouldn't keep me safe?"

"No, I'm not saying that. But I appreciate Pyotr coming along. It means I can pay more attention to you without worrying about everything around us."

"Smooth," I say and shake my head.

Pyotr maintains a discreet presence while Brandon and I walk down the sidewalk.

"Have you been to Riverside Park yet?"

"Yes. Alex brought me here when I desperately needed a quiet place amid all the chaos. Now, Pyotr and I come here for our afternoon runs."

"It's one of my favorite parts of the Upper West Side." We stop at a bench overlooking the water. "Care to sit and watch the sunset?"

"I'd love to."

Several other people had the same idea and have gathered at the water's edge. The sun is just beginning to disappear behind the buildings across the river. Hues of orange and purple are painted across the sky. The reflection on the water is breathtaking.

"I'd like to get to know you better," Brandon says, surprising me. "I've already talked to Alex and got his permission."

Now, the odd events of tonight all make sense. There was no emergency. That was Alex's made-up excuse so Brandon and I could spend time alone together.

"That was very unexpected. I'm not sure what to say." My heart is pounding.

"I know you have a lot of big changes coming up. I don't want to stress you out. We can take things as slowly as you need." He pauses. "I'd like the opportunity to get to know you better. If you'd be open to it?"

"And you're sure Alex is okay with this?"

"I'm positive. But if you'd feel better discussing it with him first, that's okay, too."

I don't know what the right answer is. Alex and I didn't discuss how he'd like me to handle this. "I'm not against it, but I'd like to talk to Alex about it before I give you a definite answer."

"I can respect that."

"Thank you." I smile, feeling much more at ease.

Once the sun sets, we slowly walk back to the apartment.

When we arrive, Viktor, Pyotr, and Alex are at the table eating.

"Thank you again for cooking," Alex says when he sees me. "The stroganoff is wonderful. It tastes just like Irina's."

"You're welcome. I love cooking."

"I wish I had known that weeks ago." He laughs.

"Thanks for letting me borrow her, Montgomery."

"Anytime. Within reason."

"I had a great time tonight," Brandon says.

"Me, too."

"Do you need a ride home?" Viktor asks. "I can drive you home."

"Nah, I'll take the subway."

I watch as Brandon walks toward the elevator and steps inside. When he turns back to face me, the smile on his face nearly makes my knees give out. But I force myself to maintain my composure. When I lead with my heart, I tend to get in trouble. This time, I'm determined to think things through before I act on them. Who knows. Maybe it'll lead to a better result. Only time will tell.

Brandon

I grab a seat in the near-empty subway car and pop my headphones in so I can try to figure out where things went wrong tonight. I thought Svetlana and I were getting along well. I could've sworn there were the beginnings of a connection. Could I have imagined it? Maybe I misread the cues because when I asked to get to know her better, she froze. I fear Svetlana's complexities exceed what anyone suspects. I don't think I could walk away if I tried, and that worries me. I don't want to repeat the sins of my past.

I was the luckiest guy in the world. It's what I thought every day after Celia Baldwin, the prettiest girl at Fort Hamilton High School, agreed to be my girlfriend. Even though I'd lost my virginity long before I met her, I was honored she chose me to be her first. I might have been a teenager, but I was a kinky bastard who liked to be in control in and out of the bedroom. Lucky for me, Celia was open to experimenting.

After graduation, I got a job as a bartender at a popular bar in Manhattan. That's where I first met Angel. He and I often worked the same shift and would go out after work. One weekend, he invited me to go to Chains. I'd never heard of it, but I assumed it was another NYC nightclub.

I was wrong. Chains was a BDSM club. That night, my eyes were opened to a whole new world that I didn't know existed. It was a world where everything I liked to do was on full display. The air smelled like sex, which was no surprise because that's exactly what was happening in every corner of the seedy club.

Celia and I quickly became regulars. She was agreeable to doing anything and everything I wanted. I loved parading my submissive's flawless body in front of the club attendees. We often fucked while others watched. Knowing men were getting off watching her didn't bother me.

Then, I started getting asked if others could join. Hell yeah. Countless nights I fucked Celia at the same time as another man. Sometimes, I'd invite women to join us. Other nights, I stayed on the sideline and watched others use her. Celia never said no. She got off on it as much as I did.

Celia was not only insatiable, she also loved pain—and I loved giving it to her. But she quickly outgrew the things I felt confident doing to her. Fortunately for us, there were plenty of other Dominants in the club who were more experienced and willing to take a scene to the next level for her.

One night, we went down to the dungeon to do a private scene with Diablo, a club regular, and a master with a bullwhip. Everything was planned beforehand, and I was confident nothing could go wrong. I bound her wrists together while Diablo bound her legs to a spreader bad. We placed her on her hands and knees. It was a challenging position.

I started the scene with a flogger to warm her up while Diablo stimulated her nipples. It didn't take long before her arousal was dripping down her leg. Then we switched places. He took a few practice swings with his whip before turning to Celia. Over and over, his whip landed on her skin. Her moans grew louder. I was so fucking hard and couldn't wait any longer.

Freeing my erection, I ordered her to open her mouth. I wasn't slow or gentle as I thrust into her. Diablo dropped his whip and began to fuck her ass, just like we had planned. I wasn't thinking clearly. I didn't realize he—

My phone vibrates in my hand, pulling my attention out of the past.

Alex: How did everything go tonight?

Me: I don't know.

Alex: What do you mean you don't know?

Me: Didn't she talk to you?

Alex: Viktor and Pyotr are still here, so we haven't had a chance to talk.

Me: I asked her, but she said she'd get back to me.

Alex: That's odd, even for Lana. I'll talk to her and let you know.

Me: Sounds good. I'll see you in the morning.

Svetlana

"LET ME KNOW WHEN YOU'RE DONE EATING. I'LL BE IN my room," I say, leaving the men to finish dinner. I really need to talk to Alex, but not until we're alone. While I wait, I grab the book I'm reading. I want to finish it before the term starts and I have to put all my time and energy into textbooks and school assignments. Unfortunately, I can't seem to focus on the words and make no progress.

"Got a few minutes?"

"Sure. Come in." Alex steps into the room but leaves the door open. I set my book aside. "Did you know what Brandon was going to ask me tonight?"

"I did," he says as he sits in the chair across from my bed.

"And you didn't think to give me a heads up?"

"I thought about it and decided not to."

"Seriously?"

"Yes, seriously." He crosses his arms.

"I would've liked a heads up."

"Think about it. If I told you he wanted to spend more time with you but decided not to ask, you'd be crushed. I didn't want you to get hurt."

I study him for a minute, weighing his words. "I guess you're right."

"Can you say that a little louder?" He grins.

I toss a pillow at him. "No. That was all you're getting." We share a laugh.

"So, what's up with you not answering him?"

"I thought you'd be happy I'm coming to you first."

"I didn't say I wasn't happy."

"And they say women are confusing."

"What's that supposed to mean?" He raises an eyebrow.

"The whole trust you and ask you first bit. I was trying to do the right thing and come to you first. But now you're wondering why I didn't give him an answer."

"Brandon already asked me for permission. I thought you'd get the hint when I left the two of you alone for dinner."

"I might've if your excuse for leaving didn't sound so real." It's not uncommon for Papa to call Alex with an emergency that needs to be handled immediately. Instead of seeing Brandon's intent, I was too busy worrying about what might be happening. "I don't know if now's a good time to do this."

"Why not?" Alex asks, genuinely concerned.

"There's a lot of big changes about to happen. Should I be adding more to the mix?"

"It's completely your decision, but if it makes a difference, I think you'll be able to handle it just fine."

"Why him and not any of the other Dominants at the club?"

"Do you not like him?"

"I mean, he seems very nice, and we have more in common than I'd realized."

"Brandon and I have been friends for years. I can tell you that you'd be completely safe with him."

"I don't question my safety with him."

"Then, what's the hesitation? Is it because he's black?"

"What? No. Brandon's your best friend. You know how badly I screwed things up last time."

"And you're afraid you're going to do it again." I nod. "It seems you have two choices. You can let the fear of making another mistake keep you from trying again, but who knows what you might miss. Or you can take that first terrifying step and see what the possibilities are."

"You really think Brandon and I might be a good match?"

"You can be a pain in the ass sometimes," he chuckles. "But yes, I think you and Brandon would get along quite well."

"Do you have his number?"

"I do."

"Do you think it would be okay if I called him?"

"I'm sure he'd like that."

Alex texts me Brandon's number and then leaves my room. I fall back onto the pillows, picturing the incredibly sexy man I spent the evening with. There's a quiet confidence about Brandon. He's a Dominant, but he's soft-spoken and kind. He too, is settled in his career, but his work is directly involved with Jelena's Hope—it feels familiar.

I've heard from the other submissives that Brandon's a master with his whip. That's something that appeals to me. I've often imagined what it would feel like to be bound and whipped. While training at Noire, I enjoyed playing with a Dominant whose implement of choice was a whip. Even though it was a very short and controlled scene, I loved every second. He had expressed an interest in being more than play partners for a night, but Czarenah didn't feel I was ready for a dynamic yet. I resented her for that judgment call, but looking back, she was right.

Exploring that side of Brandon might be fun. But as excited as I am for the possibilities a dynamic brings, I'm equally as nervous. I have a history of screwing up anything good in my life, of pushing away people who get too close before they can hurt me.

Now, I'm face to face with the opportunity to submit to a man, a Dominant, who is worthy of my submission. But can I do this the right way, or will I screw this up like I do everything else? For both our sakes, I hope I can do this.

My hands shake as I input his number and tap the green call icon. The phone rings several times. Just when I think it's going to voicemail, he picks up.

"Hello?"

"Brandon?"

"Yeah."

"It's Svetlana."

"Hi."

"Alex gave me your number. I hope that was okay."

"Of course. I'm glad you called."

"I had a chance to talk to Alex."

"Okay."

"If you're still open to it, I'd like to get to know you. To see if we might work as a Dom/sub couple."

"I'm glad to hear that."

"I have one request."

"What is it?"

"Can we take things slowly?"

"*Mon petit papillon*, we can do this however you need."

Svetlana is learning what it means to submit, but trust doesn't come easily. Will she give Brandon her heart—or will she run before he can claim it? Continue their story in *Fractured Lives*.

Also by Tara Conrad

Find Tara's Books Here

About Tara

Tara Conrad is the author behind sizzling and passionate love stories that ignite the senses. Her novels celebrate the fiery intensity of desire. They're known for having a blend of deep emotional connections, relatable characters, and captivating plots that ensnare readers from the very first page to the last.

Tara's married to her soulmate and Dominant, George. They are about to celebrate their 30th anniversary and are more in love today than yesterday. George encouraged Tara to start writing, and with each passing day, she's more thankful for his insistence that she tell her stories and his partnership on this journey. There's no one else in this world she'd ever want by her side. He is her happily ever after.

Acknowledgments

First and foremost, I want to thank my husband, George. Without your support and encouragement, I could never do any of this. I'm in awe of your dedication to making sure I can pursue my dreams. I don't know how you manage to go from your day job to your second job as my do-it-all man, but I'm eternally thankful. I love you forever and a day.

George, Jacob, Kayla, Rebekah, and Jonathan: Thank you all for being my cheerleaders. Knowing I have all of your support means the world to me.

Dana H.- You knew Brandon and Lana's story before I found the courage to say it out loud. I know it's deeply personal to you, me, and so many other women. I'm going to do my very best to honor this storyline.

To all my Beta and ARC readers: You all are AMAZE-BALLS! I will never grow tired of getting your messages of support and love. It's because of each of you that I continue to write in the Fire and Ice World. I hope you continue to love reading the books as much as I love writing them!

www.ingramcontent.com/pod-product-compliance
Lightning Source LLC
Chambersburg PA
CBHW061530310726
48972CB00008B/2399